## THE DOUBLE FUDGE DARE

"You have to eat the *whole* cake. Right now. I double-dare you," my sister Meg said smugly.

Bart stared at the four layers of chocolate cake, then grinned.

"Eat it! Eat it!" the crowd began to chant.

Bart broke off a huge chunk and stuffed it in his mouth. "Ummm, good," he said with his mouth full.

Chunk followed chunk. I began to feel sick just watching him! Bart's face was smeared with chocolate, and his eyes were beginning to get kind of wild. . . .

# The Double Fudge Dare

## Louise Ladd

A BANTAM SKYLARK BOOK®
NEW YORK · TORONTO · LONDON · SYDNEY · AUCKLAND

RL 4, 008–012

THE DOUBLE FUDGE DARE
*A Bantam Skylark Book / March 1989*

*Skylark Books is a registered trademark of Bantam Books, a division of Bantam
Doubleday Dell Publishing Group, Inc. Registered in U.S. Patent and Trademark
Office and elsewhere.*

ISBN 0-553-15684-5

*Published simultaneously in the United States and Canada*

Bantam Books are published by Bantam Books, a division of Bantam Doubleday Dell
Publishing Group, Inc. Its trademark, consisting of the words "Bantam Books" and
the portrayal of a rooster, is Registered in U.S. Patent and Trademark Office and in
other countries. Marca Registrada. Bantam Books, 666 Fifth Avenue, New York
10103.

PRINTED IN THE UNITED STATES OF AMERICA

S     0 9 8 7 6 5 4 3

For Jean Mercier

And for Alida, Ann, Betty L., Betty R.,
Bob, Bobbie, Carolyn B., Carolyn S., Cath-
erine, Chris, Darcy, Dulcey, Jane, Kay,
Lucy, Nancy, and Susan

With love

# The
# Double
# Fudge Dare

# 1

Of course, you could say the trouble started the day we moved in next door to the Brats. Or the day the Zoning Board said Babba couldn't live with us. But the *major* trouble started that day on the beach, the day the first flamingo arrived.

I'd just picked up a tiny white shell with half-numb fingers—the beach gets kind of chilly in October—when I looked up and saw my sister, Meg, down by the jetty talking to someone. I squinted my eyes to see better. Oh shoot, I thought, that isn't just somebody, it's *Bratty Bart*.

I stuffed the shells I'd collected in my towel and took off toward them at a run.

"I'll throw this jellyfish right in your face!" Meg was shouting.

"You don't have the guts to touch that thing." Bratty Bart flashed his cocky grin.

"Oh, yeah?" Meg began to snap her fingers, the way she always does when she's mad.

"Yeah. Girls don't like slimy stuff." He nudged the dead jellyfish with the toe of his sneaker. It jiggled like a lump of pale Jell-O. "I dare you to pick it up."

Whoops, here we go, I thought. "Dare" was a magic word to Meg.

She looked at the glop on the sand, then at Bart.

He laughed. "Go on. Pick it up. I double-dare you."

In one smooth motion Meg scooped up the jellyfish and whipped it into his grinning face.

"Blahhhhhhhgh!" Bart screamed. The smell of rotten fish exploded into the air. Bart's face was plastered with the slimy stuff. Gobs of goo clung to his eyebrows, his cheeks, his hair. He scrubbed at his face like crazy, spitting out bits of sand and yuck.

Meg had done it again.

I felt kind of sorry for Bart and handed him my towel, forgetting about my shells.

"I'll get you for this!" he sputtered. He threw the towel in the air. Shells flew all over the beach.

"You jerk!" I shouted. "Look what you did!"

He ignored me. "Just you wait!" he yelled at Meg. "Just you wait! You'll be sorry! I'll get you good!" He turned and galloped up the beach toward the dunes.

"Did you see his face?" Meg crowed. "That'll teach him not to mess with me!"

I watched Bart Bradley disappear over the top of the dune. He was such a pain. Most of the girls in sixth grade thought he was cute, with those dark blue eyes and pale blond hair, but they didn't have to live next door to him.

Meg was flapping her hands in the air. "Did the jellyfish sting you?" I asked.

"No, it's not the stinging kind, I guess. Or maybe they can't sting when they're dead. But it feels *gross*!" She jogged down to the edge of the water to wash her hands. This was tricky because although the waves were small, they rolled in fast, one after the other. Meg is quick on her feet, but a wavelet or two managed to catch her.

I stood there watching her, shivering a little. Never in a million years could I pick up a dead jellyfish. Meg was probably the only person in the world who would.

You'd never guess we were twins. We were as different as tacos and egg rolls.

I was the egg roll. Mom said it was because I was "maturing" a little faster than Meg, but I felt like I was made of little bits of a million different things—shrimp, cabbage, and lots of stuff I couldn't name. I was also kind of on the round side, pleasingly plump, my father called it.

Even my hair was the color of a crispy egg roll—in the summer. In winter it faded to boring brown. Meg's was coppery red. It stayed the same all year round, and so did Meg. She was definitely a taco, her bits and pieces all blended in a hot spicy sauce, tucked into a smooth shell. I love tacos, but living with one isn't always easy.

She jogged back to me. "Let's go, Kit. It's getting late. We promised Mom we'd start dinner."

"Oh yeah, I forgot." I started up toward the path.

"Don't forget your towel."

"Oh yeah, right." I changed direction.

"Like Babba says, you'd forget your head if it weren't attached," she teased.

Babba is our grandmother. She has a quote for every situation, and that's only one of the great things about her. I grabbed up my towel and looked around in case some of my shells had landed nearby.

"Hurry *up*, Kit," Meg called. "My feet are freezing."

I scooped up a couple of jingle shells and trotted back to her. "You know," I said, "you wouldn't have wet feet if you'd washed your hands with sand the way the Arabs do."

She stared at me. "Where'd you hear *that*?"

I shrugged. "It was in a book."

"You sure read the weirdest things." Meg

couldn't understand why I loved books so much. I couldn't understand why she loved soccer so much.

I looked at her empty hands. "Didn't you bring a towel to the beach, too?"

"Oh yeah, I forgot." She hurried to get it.

I grinned and called after her, "You'd forget your head if it weren't attached." She pretended not to hear.

"How come you made us bring towels?" she asked, coming back. "I told you it was too cold for swimming."

"It was so bright and warm earlier, I thought maybe."

We started up the path over the dune. "Meg?" I asked. "Do you always have to get in fights with boys?"

"Sure. Why not?" she said cheerfully.

"It's just that I was hoping, well . . . now that we've moved to a new town, maybe we could sort of, you know, fit in better. Not be so different all the time."

"I *like* being different." She tossed her towel in the air and caught it, then she must have noticed the way I looked. "Hey, Kit, come on, we just moved here a month ago and we already have lots of friends."

"Yeah, but no one special, like we had Liz and Sarah back in Treaton. And see, there's this one girl in my class, Katy Stillson, and she has this friend Jennifer, and I like them and they asked me to sit with them at lunch last week . . ."

"Then what's the problem?"

"Well, Katy's so *normal*, and so is Jennifer. I mean, they *like* boys. They don't get mad and fight with them all the time."

"I don't fight with boys *all* the time. Besides," Meg went on, "you'll get mad too when you hear what Bratty Bart said."

Bart was always saying things that made Meg explode. The day we moved in, Meg found out that Bart and his brother Brett were named after some cowboys on an old TV show. Naturally she gave them a hard time about it, so they began calling her Nut-Meg to get even. Worse, they called me Kitty, as in "Here, Kitty, Kitty, Kitty."

They were total pains. Like when we put up our old tent in the backyard, they said it was gross. And the one time we tried to sleep out in it, they pulled up all the stakes in the middle of the night and the whole thing fell down and woke us up and we screamed, and then the whole neighborhood woke up. And *then*, boy, were we in trouble.

"What did Bart say this time?" I asked as we reached the road. "Was it your hair again?"

Bart claimed Meg's hair was so red it glowed in the dark like a candle. He liked to sneak up and pull her hair, then pretend he'd gotten burned. He was such a dip.

"It wasn't my hair," Meg said. "It was Will."

"Will?" He was our little brother. "What about him?"

"Bart said we were turning him into a wimp."

"*A wimp?!*"

"Can you believe it? He said Will was old enough to ride a two-wheeler now instead of a baby bike, and he should be going out for Midget soccer, and he and Brett would teach him how to play."

"He's got a lot of nerve!"

"My soccer team almost made the state championships last year." Meg began to snap her fingers, so I knew she was getting mad all over again. "I could teach Will better than those jerks could."

"Besides," I added, "Will's too young for a two-wheeler. He's just started first grade." I could hardly believe Will was already in school. I still thought of him as a chubby little toddler, strutting around in droopy diapers.

Meg nodded. "He could fall off and hurt himself."

Meg and I had helped take care of Will ever since he was born. We did everything for him. We fed him, gave him baths, took him for rides, read to him, even taught him his numbers and letters. It was like having a real live doll to play with.

We had almost reached our house when something that had been nagging at the back of my mind suddenly jumped out in front. "Guess what?" I said. "We've been so busy talking about Will—"

"—that we forgot to pick him up," Meg finished for me. When Will played over at his friend Georgie's house we always walked him home. "I'll go get him," she said quickly. "You start dinner."

"I hate starting dinner." This was one of our new chores since Mom began working full-time. I didn't mind *helping* with dinner but, somehow, *starting* it seemed like the kind of thing mothers should do, not kids.

"I hate it, too," Meg said. "Besides, I'm a lousy cook."

That was true. Last week Meg had made a crunchy tuna casserole—she forgot to cook the noodles first! I practically broke a tooth on it.

"You just want to go to the Kirstens," I told her. So did I. Mrs. Kirsten was a terrific cook and she always insisted we try an apple tart or a home-made granola bar while Will helped Georgie put away the toys they'd been playing with. Will showed very good taste when he chose Georgie as his best friend.

"Okay, I'll toss you for it," Meg said. "What do you want, odds or evens?"

"Odds."

"Ready? One, two, three!"

She put out one finger. Added to my one made two.

Meg flew up the street. I headed slowly for the house.

Mom would be home from the advertising agency soon, probably tired. She wasn't used to working full-time yet.

I shuffled through a drift of red and gold leaves along our street. If she and Dad weren't divorced, she wouldn't have to work. But I was glad the fighting was over, even though it sure changed our lives around. Dad's company had transferred him to Atlanta and we only saw him when he came back on business trips—although that was pretty often. Then we'd moved from our big old house in Treaton to this little beach house. The beach part was great, but the house was so small it only had one bathroom. Still the hardest thing to get used to was Mom working full-time.

I kicked a pile of leaves and a swirl of red, brown, and gold fluttered in the air.

"Here, Kitty, Kitty, Kitty!"

I whirled around. "Cut that out!"

Brett leaned on his rake, his hair as blond as his brother's, his eyes the same deep blue. Those two looked more like twins than Meg and I did, although Brett was a year older, in junior high.

But there was something different—special— about Brett. Mostly he was a pain, but once in a while, just for a moment, he stirred up all those different little parts of me, leaving me breathless and mixed-up. Like I felt right now.

He grinned. "What's the matter, Puss-Puss? Your fur get ruffled?"

"What do you want?" I snapped, confused.

"Put your claws back in. I just want you to give Nutty-Meg a message."

"What message?"

"Tell her I said to lay off my brother." His grin faded.

I immediately went back to feeling normal—and annoyed. "She only did what Bart dared her to do. Besides, your brother has no right to insult *our* brother."

"He was just trying to help."

"Tell him to mind his own business."

"You and your sister treat Will like a baby. You're turning him into a wimp."

Fireworks went off inside me. "He's *not* a wimp! And what do you care anyway? It's none of your business!"

"It's because—" He stopped himself. "Oh, never mind." He grabbed the rake and stalked off toward his garage.

I stared after him, Roman candles still sizzling around in me. Then I said a swear word Mom never let us say, stomped down our driveway, and pounded up the back porch steps.

Meg was right. Those Brats were nothing but total jerks.

# 2

My key stuck in the lock so I used a few more swears to get it out and kicked open the door.

The kitchen was dim and chilly. Lady, our mostly-collie mutt, wagged her tail at me but didn't bother to get up. It was awful to come home like this. Before Mom had to work, the house would be warm, filled with the smells of dinner cooking.

Hansel and Gretel, Will's goldfish, were swimming around in their plastic bowl on the kitchen counter. Will moved them to a different place every day so they wouldn't get "bored."

"You dumb fish sure have it lucky," I said,

dragging the macaroni pot out of the cupboard. "Swim, swim, swim, that's all you have to do. No one ever asks *you* to start dinner."

I filled the pot with water and put it on to boil, then attacked the woodstove. I scrunched newspapers into balls and added kindling. "No one insults your little brother, either," I added, tossing in a couple of logs.

Lady cocked an ear at me when I lit the fire and clanked the door shut. "You, too, Lady. All you do is lie around and wait for someone to take care of you." I poured dog food into her bowl. "If Babba was here, I'd have someone to take care of *me*."

Babba was supposed to be here. She was supposed to move up from Florida and live with us. There wasn't room in the house, but we were going to fix an apartment for her over the garage. Then, after we moved in, the Zoning Board—whoever they were—told us we couldn't build the apartment. I couldn't see why not. After all, it was *our* house.

Meg had wasted that jellyfish. The Zoning Board were the ones who deserved a stinky, slimy blob of gunk.

Maybe I should go down to the beach and collect a bunch of jellyfish to throw at the Zoning Board. One from Meg, one from me, one from Will, and the fattest, squishiest one from Mom. Mom wanted Babba here even more than I did. Besides being her mother, Babba was also Mom's best friend. Plus, Mom needed Babba. Her job kept her busy all week, then all weekend she shopped and cleaned and ran errands. Babba loved to do that kind of stuff and Mom didn't have time.

The doorbell rang. Lady raced to the front door, barking like crazy, just as the macaroni water boiled over. Smoke was seeping out of the woodstove. I must have forgotten to open the damper.

"Just a minute!" I yelled to the door. I grabbed the macaroni pot off the stove and it crashed into the fishbowl. Hansel and Gretel went sailing onto the floor, along with a ton of water. Their plastic bowl rolled under the kitchen table.

"Help!" I dropped the macaroni pot and hot water splashed all over the counter. I decided to ignore it and scrambled under the table after the bowl, soaking my jeans in fish water.

The doorbell rang again. "I'm coming! I'm coming!" I grabbed the bowl, backed out—banging my head—then raced to the sink and ran some water into it quickly. The woodsmoke was getting thick. Lady was still barking her head off.

Hansel, the spotted fish, had flopped his way over to the refrigerator. I swooped him up. He felt yucky—all wet and tickly—in my hand. I ran back to the sink, plopped him in the bowl, then grabbed it up and looked around for Gretel.

A tiny gold tail stuck out from under the stove. I started for her, then the kitchen floor suddenly turned into a skating rink. One foot went out from under me, then the other. I crashed down on my rear end.

The bowl flew one way, Hansel flew the other.

The doorbell rang again. "Can't you see this is an emergency?!" I yelled. I crawled over to the bowl, then crept up on Hansel. "Don't move now, that's a good fish." He flopped twice and I grabbed him.

Gretel had wriggled her way out from under the stove. Still on my hands and knees, I made my way over to where she lay gasping. I scooped her into the bowl and crawled back to the sink.

I stood up carefully, clutching the bowl to my chest. The smoke was thicker up there. The doorbell rang again and Lady went into a new burst of barking.

"I'm coming! I'm coming! *I'm coming!*" I shouted, splashing water into the bowl. Hanging on to the counter in case my feet turned into ice skates again, I made my way over to the woodstove, opened the damper, and finally reached the safety of the living room rug. I felt like I'd just climbed Mount Everest without an oxygen mask.

Lady was still attacking the front door. I grabbed her collar before I opened it. Good thing I did because it was the UPS man. She hates UPS for some reason.

"Package for the Sullivans. Sign here." He held out a clipboard. How was I supposed to sign anything when my hands were full of crazy Lady? You'd have thought she was after a grizzly bear.

Finally I got a grip on her collar with my left hand, snaked my right hand out through a hole in the screen door, and scribbled my name in the little space he pointed to.

The UPS man looked me up and down. "Been swimming?"

"Yes, on the kitchen floor."

He stared at me.

"Chasing goldfish," I added.

He changed the subject. "I'll just leave this outside for now," he said, looking at Lady. I noticed the package for the first time. It was big. "Dogs hate me. Don't know why. I got two at home and they like me fine. Maybe it's the uniform."

"Maybe," I said.

"Have a good day." He strolled back to his truck and drove off.

Whoever invented "Have a good day" was weird. Didn't they know most people have terrible days, like the one I was having now?

"What's going on here?" Mom called from the kitchen. "Kit? Meg? There's water all over the floor and this place is full of smoke!" She came into the living room, limping a little in her high heels.

"I'll mop up, as soon as I open the windows," I mumbled.

She took a good look at me. "What happened? You're soaked."

"Ah, you could say Hansel and Gretel went for a walk—or a flop."

"It wouldn't be the first time." She pushed her

hair back. "I'm glad I finally found that plastic bowl for them. Are they all right?"

"I think so. But if they don't make it, I'll buy Will some more," I said, opening windows.

"Don't open all of them. It's getting cold out. Did you forget the damper again?" She kicked off her shoes and collapsed on the couch with a groan. Mom was slim, with nice long legs and dark red hair that curled around her face. I hoped to inherit her long legs—some day.

"I'm going to kill him!" Meg yelled from the kitchen. Will sprinted into the living room and made a flying leap for Mom. He almost squashed her when he landed in her lap.

"What did Will do?" Mom asked, hugging him.

"Not Will! *Bratty Bart!*" Meg appeared in the doorway. She was frosted with shaving cream from head to foot. Foamy white swirls and spatters coated her hair, her new jacket, her jeans. A strong smell of fake lemon surrounded her.

Mom began to laugh.

"It's not funny!" Meg shouted. "He's going to pay for this! He'd better watch out! This is war!"

# 3

"Calm down, Meg," Mom said, still laughing. "Tell us what happened."

"My new jacket," Meg wailed. "He's ruined it."

"It'll wash out."

"I'm going to kill him! He ambushed me! No warning! Nothing!"

"He warned *me*, Meg," Will said, curling up in Mom's lap. "He told me to run. And I did! I runned fast!"

"Ran, I *ran*," Mom automatically corrected him. "What did you do to Bart, Meg?"

17

"Nothing! Well . . . almost nothing." She began to wilt a little.

"Tell me about it while I fix dinner." Mom eased Will off her lap and stood up.

"The macaroni—I forgot," I said.

"It's all right, you tried," Mom answered. She wrinkled her nose as she got closer to Meg. "On second thought, you'd better take a shower first, Meg, and put your clothes in the washing machine. Kit, you'd better change into something dry."

"What about the box?" Will said.

"What box?" Meg asked.

"The big one. On the front porch."

"Oh, the UPS! I forgot!" I ran to the door and yanked it open. The package was about four feet tall, but wasn't heavy. I brought it in and looked at the label. "It's from Babba!"

"How come?" Meg asked. "It's nobody's birthday."

"What is it? What is it?" Will bounced up and down.

"Open it and see," Mom said, smiling. I could tell Babba had already told her about it.

"It's for Kit and me," Meg told Will, ripping open the top. He deflated like a balloon. "But we'll share it with you," she added, giving him a hug.

Just inside the box I saw a white envelope with Babba's handwriting on it. "There's a card. You have to open the card first," I said.

"Later." She pulled out wads of crumpled newspaper.

"No, first."

"You open it," she said, waving the card at me.

"Then you have to wait." I clamped my hand down on top of the box.

"Cut that out!"

"Yackety yack," Will sang up high, then tried to fake a deep voice. "Don't talk back."

We all broke up. Will hated anyone to fight. He'd heard that silly song on the radio and discovered he could stop any argument because we'd all dissolve in giggles when he tried to sing it.

It was hard to have a decent fight with Will around the house.

Meg left the package alone and I ripped open the envelope. Inside there was one of those romantic photo cards with a picture of flamingos outlined against a beautiful sunset. The printed message said, "Thinking of you," and Babba had added: "For my favorite granddaughters, a silly something from Florida to liven up your new house. I'm sure you'll think of a good use for it. Hugs and kisses to little Will, too."

The moment I stopped reading, Meg began yanking out more newspapers. "It's something pink," she announced.

"What is it? What is it?" Will asked.

"Don't get shaving cream on it," I warned.

Slowly Meg pulled a pink object out of the box.

"It's a bird!" Will shouted.

"It's a flamingo," I told him. "See? Like on the card."

"Can it fly?" he asked.

"No, it's plastic."

"How come Babba sent us a pink, plastic pla-mingo?"

"*Fla*-mingo," Mom corrected him. She turned to Meg and me. "Babba said there was a motel going out of business near where she works, and she just couldn't resist buying one. She said she was actu-ally tempted to buy the whole flock—there were at least thirty of them—but she thought that would be a bit much."

"Yeah," I said. "Even one is a bit much." The flamingo was almost four feet tall and a bright, putrid pink. It had rods coming from the bottom of the feet, so you could stick it in a lawn, I guess.

"We got a pink, plastic plamingo," Will chanted. "A pink, plastic plamingo."

"*Fla*-mingo," I said automatically, but I smiled at him. He was so cute when he mispronounced words. "What are we going to do with it?"

Meg had been studying the thing carefully. "I'm not sure—yet—but I think Babba has just sent us the first weapon in our war against Bratty Bart."

Fortunately Meg had a lot of social studies homework that night, so she couldn't devote much time to the Brat War. As soon as I finished my math, I called Babba. That was one of our birthday presents from her; we could call her as often as we liked and she'd pay for it.

"Hello?" Babba's TV was loud in the background.

"Hi, Babba! It's me, Kit. Thanks for the flamingo."

"It came? Oh, good." The TV noise vanished. "I hope you like it."

"Sure we do. It's really . . . uh, really . . . pink."

Babba chuckled. "I'm not sure what you'll do with it. It's a little large for a Christmas tree decoration."

I pictured the flamingo perched on top of our tree and giggled. "Actually, Meg is working on a plan for it right now. If she's finished her homework. You know what that kid next door did? Bratty Bart? He sprayed Meg all over with shaving cream."

"What did Meg do to *him*?" You could tell Babba knew Meg pretty well.

"Nothing. She only took his dare." I told her about the jellyfish and my shells.

"That child just loves to make waves, doesn't she?" Babba laughed. I could see her in my mind, sitting in her favorite white wicker chair, her long, slender legs propped on her needlepoint footstool, her cat, Daffodil, asleep on her lap.

Suddenly I missed her so much it hurt. "Babba,

*why* can't you move up here? We could find you an apartment."

"Oh, darling." She became serious immediately. "I thought you understood. If we could have built a place over the garage, I could have managed."

"I *miss* you, Babba. I want you to live with us. Besides, we need you."

"I know, darling, I want to be with you, too. When the Zoning Board turned us down, your mother looked into finding me an apartment, but rents in your area of Connecticut are simply ridiculous. I just couldn't afford it."

"But you have a lot of money," I said. "You're always sending us neat presents—weird sometimes, but neat—" Babba laughed. "And you pay for the phone calls, and you wear nice clothes . . ."

"Kit, darling, I don't spend much on clothes. My friends call me Barbara the Bargain Hunter. Also, during my modeling days, I learned a lot about style—that's really the secret to looking well dressed."

"You ought to be a model now," I said. It was true. Babba was still beautiful, tall and slim, with pure white hair, and only two tiny little varicose veins in the back of one leg.

"No, thanks," she said. "Modeling is a hard way to earn a living. What I should have done is learn a trade. Then I wouldn't be a salesperson in a jewelry store now. But in my day, we weren't raised to have careers. We thought being a wife and mother was enough." She sighed.

Babba had been lonely ever since Grandpop died, Mom had told us. She had lots of friends down in Florida, but she really missed having a family to take care of. It would have been so perfect if we could have built that apartment.

"Oh, well," Babba continued. "Que sera, sera. What will be, will be. I'm glad you like the flamingo. It was just too wild and wonderful to pass up."

"Was it expensive?" I asked cautiously.

"Oh, no! The postage cost more than it did. Now, don't you worry, one of my greatest pleasures is buying presents for my grandchildren."

After I hung up, I sat there staring at the flamingo, thinking hard. Meg wanted to get back at Bratty Bart. I wanted Babba. I came to a decision. I went upstairs to the room Meg and I shared. She looked up from her homework when I opened the door.

"Forget Bratty Bart," I told her. "We need to use that flamingo to fight the Zoning Board."

"How?" Meg asked.

"I don't know yet. As soon as you finish your homework we can come up with a plan."

"But what about Bratty Bart?"

"Babba sent us the flamingo. It's only fair to use *her* flamingo to help her move up here. Besides, you'll think of something else for Bart . . . if you *have* to get back at him."

"Of course I have to get back at him!" Meg snapped her fingers so fast it sounded like corn popping.

I knew it was hopeless, but I made one last try.

"Seems to me, you're even. One can of shaving cream versus one dead jellyfish."

"Kit!" She sounded totally shocked. "He dared me!"

I sighed and gave up. If Meg wanted a Brat War, a war there would be. Meantime, I had my own problems.

"Okay," I said, "but listen, Meg, you've got to help me. Besides wanting Babba, we really *need* her." I told her about Hansel and Gretel, the flying goldfish. "That wouldn't have happened if Babba was here, and the woodstove wouldn't have smoked up the whole house either."

"Are the fish all right?" she asked.

"Sure. I've checked them about every five minutes tonight and they're swimming around like always. Maybe the exercise was good for them."

Meg frowned. "It sure would be nice to have Babba here. But I don't see how one little flamingo—"

"It's not so little."

"Okay, one huge flamingo is going to solve the problem."

"Meg, you've got to help me come up with a plan."

"All right, I'll help you if you'll help me." She had That Look in her eye.

"Help you with Bratty Bart?" I asked suspiciously.

"Of course!"

I should have known better. After eleven years

with Meg I *should* have known there was no telling what kind of trouble she'd drag me into. I *should* have kept my mouth shut. Instead I said slowly, "It's a deal."

"Great! But not tonight. We'll go to the beach after school tomorrow and come up with a plan for Babba. Right now you have to quiz me on the capital cities of South America."

We had a half day of school because of a teachers' convention, so we got to the beach early the next afternoon.

A lot of people only like the beach when it's warm and sunny, but Meg and I love it in all kinds of weather. Today it was cold, with bumpy gray clouds overhead. The tide was out, leaving a wide stretch of damp, rippled sand. The jetties, those long piles of jumbled rocks that poked out into the Sound, were bare.

"It's a lot easier to get back at Bratty Bart than to come up with an idea for Babba," Meg said, winging a mussel shell into the flat water.

"Let's talk about Bart later." *Much* later, I thought.

"I just don't see how a silly plastic bird is going to make the Zoning Board change its mind."

"I told you, I don't either," I said. "It just has to, that's all."

"What can a couple of kids do when it comes to government things like the Zoning Board?"

I picked up a yellow jingle shell. Running my

finger over its smooth, pearly inside I said, "There must be something. Think."

She thought for about two seconds. "I know, we'll call the Zoning Board and ask them how we can make them change their minds."

"You're crazy. You think they'd *tell* us?"

"I don't know." She leaped over a largish pool left behind by the tide. "What else can we do?"

I jumped over the same pool and landed in three inches of icy water. Hoping Meg hadn't noticed, I said, "Maybe we could put the flamingo on the front lawn of Town Hall, with a sign on it: 'Please let the Sullivans build an apartment over their garage.'"

"Are you kidding? I'm sure *that* would do a lot of good."

I walked along, thinking hard. We'd been to Florida a lot, to visit Babba and Grandpop. Pink, plastic flamingos weren't uncommon down there, but I'd never seen one in Connecticut. I tried to picture Florida. I thought I remembered the motel near where Babba worked, the one going out of business. Besides flamingos it had a little windmill, and fake deer, and gnomes—all kinds of plastic statues dotted around the lawn. Tacky, my father had called it. Dad was an expert on what was tasteful and what was tacky.

Tacky. Tasteful. Suddenly the answer was right there in front of me.

"I've got it! I've got it!" I called, trotting to catch up with Meg.

"Yeah? What is it?" She turned around.

"Have you ever seen a tacky motel, or a tacky house, in Connecticut?"

"I don't know. I guess not. At least not around here."

"And don't you think that the Zoning Board might think it was really tacky if we put not one, but an *entire flock* of pink flamingos on our front lawn?"

"Sure, but—"

"And don't you think the Zoning Board—and our neighbors—would rather let us build a lovely, tasteful apartment over our garage instead of having to look at an extremely tacky flock of flamingos every day?"

"What do you mean?"

"We put a whole flock of flamingos in our front yard, then when the Zoning Board complains about them, we say, 'Sure, we'll get rid of the flamingos if you let us build Babba's apartment.'"

"Kit! That's blackmail!"

"Yes, it is." I grinned.

She began to smile. "It's blackmail. And it's *beautiful*."

"*And* our tacky front yard will definitely annoy two blond neighbors whose names begin with B."

"Oh, wow! Kit, it's perfect! You're a genius!" Meg did a few cartwheels to celebrate.

I'm not into cartwheels. I just stood there on

the gray, cold beach and let warm waves of satisfaction wash over me.

Between us, Meg and I had saved up almost eighty dollars of our babysitting money. We went straight home and called Babba. If the rest of the flamingos had been sold, my beautiful plan would crumble to dust.

The owner of the jewelry store where Babba worked answered the phone but she put Babba on right away. "What's the matter? Who's hurt? Is someone sick?" Babba demanded.

"It's okay, Babba, everything's fine," I answered. "Are the rest of the flamingos still at the motel?"

"Flamingos? You call me in the middle of the day and scare me to death to ask about flamingos?"

"We're sorry, we really are," Meg said on the extension. "We didn't mean to scare you. But could you run over to the motel and buy the rest of the flamingos? We'll pay you back. It's really important."

"It must be if you called me before the rates go down at five. Tell me about it."

We explained our beautiful, perfect plan to blackmail the Zoning Board. There was a short silence when we finished, then Babba said in an odd, smothered voice, "Have you asked your mother about this?"

"Not yet. But she won't mind." It was the first

time I'd thought about Mom. I said quickly, "Do you think seventy-six dollars and thirty cents, minus the cost of this call, will be enough?"

Babba burst out laughing. "You two are the limit. I never saw such a pair," she finally managed to say.

I felt slightly insulted. I thought this was a brilliant plan.

"Babba," Meg said. "We're serious. This will work. I know it will."

Finally Babba agreed to check with the motel about the flamingos, but not before she made us promise to talk to Mom *and Dad* about it.

"*Dad?* How come?"

"Your father is helping your mother buy that house. His name is on the mortgage, so in a way it's his front lawn, too."

A really weird thing happened the minute our parents were divorced. All the shouting and yelling stopped and they began to help each other out, like with the mortgage. They seemed to be friends again. Most of the time.

"I'll call you at nine o'clock tonight," Babba continued. "And I'll want to speak to your mother personally."

"Babba!" Meg and I said together.

"I'm not saying you'd lie," she answered. "But more than once you've committed the sin of omission."

"Like when?" I asked.

"Like the time you talked your parents into letting you keep Lady and conveniently forgot to mention that she was expecting puppies."

"But, Babba, she followed us home!"

"At the end of a leash, after you paid your friend three dollars for her."

"How did you find out?" Meg asked.

"A little bird told me." That was Babba's favorite answer, and meant she wasn't going to say any more about the subject.

After we hung up, Meg joined me in the kitchen, saying, "Mom will be easy . . ."

"But Dad won't," I finished for her.

Our father is a very precise sort of person. When we lived in Treaton he kept our lawn green, the bushes trimmed, everything perfect. He's an accountant with a big corporation. He's good at his job because he's so picky about details, but this does not make him an easy person to live with.

Mom is about as opposite from him as you can get. She's what you might call a free spirit when it comes to details like doing the laundry and planning meals and remembering to pick us up on time. She'll get an idea, whip out her sketch pad, and hours later dinner will still be in the freezer, and Meg and I will be on some street corner, still waiting for her. All of which does not make her an easy person to live with either. Interesting maybe, but not easy.

"Let's wait to talk to Mom," Meg said, "until after she's had her glass of wine . . ."

". . . and a nice big dinner," I added.

"And the woodstove makes things all cozy . . ."

". . . and she's read the paper . . ."

". . . and has her slippers on, and her old bathrobe." We grinned at each other.

Then I asked, "But what about Dad?"

"Let's call him at work. That way he'll be too busy to really think about it. Besides, we can use his eight hundred number and it won't cost anything."

"Okay. You call."

"No, you. He likes you better."

"No he doesn't. You're just trying to get out of it."

"Okay, we'll both call."

Meg went back to the living room extension and I dialed his number. "It's ringing," I yelled. "Pick up."

Dad's secretary, Mrs. Fein, answered. She was all right, but she didn't seem to like kids much. She answered my question in a cool voice. "Your father's not in."

"Oh. When will he be back?" I asked.

"He's out of town until Friday."

"Hooray!" Meg shouted.

"I beg your pardon?" Mrs. Fein's voice turned frosty.

"She didn't mean anything," I said quickly.

"She, uh, she was just, uh, watching this quiz show on TV and somebody won something."

"I see." Mrs. Fein sounded as brittle as an icicle. "Would you like the number where you can reach him in Philadelphia?"

"Philadelphia? Oh no, that's too far. Dad would never approve if we ran up a big long-distance bill like that," I said, thinking of our prime-time phone call to Florida.

"Besides, it's not important," Meg added. "We, uh, just called to say hello."

"He'll be checking in with me later. I'll tell him you called."

"Oh, don't bother," I said, as light as air. "It's not important. Not important *at all.*"

"I'll tell him you called," Mrs. Fein said grimly and hung up.

I ran into the living room. "She knows something's wrong."

"We'll have to leave the phone off the hook so he can't get through."

"Mom might find it."

"We'll say Lady did it, and then take it off again when she isn't looking." Meg lifted the receiver and dropped it behind the couch.

"If you hadn't said hooray . . ."

"I couldn't help it. If Dad's out of town, Babba can't blame us if we say we couldn't reach him so we couldn't ask him."

"It's serendipity!"

"What's that mean?"

"It's a word in a book I was reading. I remembered it because it's so much fun to say. Seren-*dip*ity! It means a happy accident."

"Happy accident. I like that." Meg looked at her watch. "Just don't forget. We still have to convince Mom to let us put a flock of flamingos on the front lawn." She looked back at her watch quickly. "Oh no! We forgot to pick up Will!"

"Not again." I groaned.

We dashed for the door.

# 5

Georgie's house was two blocks up and three blocks over from ours. As we rounded the corner, we saw a tiny figure ambling toward us.

"Will!" Meg shouted. "What are you doing here all by yourself?"

He stopped and squatted down on the sidewalk until we reached him. "I'm walking myself home."

"You're too little to walk home alone," I said. "Why didn't you wait for us?"

"I got bored." He grinned, his angel smile lighting up his face. "Georgie and Mrs. Kirsten had to go to the 'mergency room."

"What happened?" Meg took Will's hand but he snatched it back.

"Georgie fell down and there was *lots* of blood." This seemed to please Will. "Georgie cried real loud."

"Why didn't you call us?"

"I did. And Mrs. Kirsten did. But there was just busy, busy, busy."

Meg and I looked at each other. We knew we'd better put the phone back on the hook as soon as we got home.

"Mrs. Kirsten gave me cookies and turned on the TV and said to wait 'cause you were coming right away but you didn't. So I walked myself. And I didn't get lost."

"No, you didn't," I said. "Because Meg and I found you. But you should have waited, Will. Promise me you won't ever try this again."

"No! I won't! I'm a big boy. I can do it myself. I'll show you." He turned around and marched off toward home, his little body full of determination.

Meg and I followed behind him. At the corner he stopped and looked up and down both streets. There was one car coming, half a block away. He waited for it to pass, then crossed the street and headed for the house. He didn't look back at us once.

"He's not old enough to walk home alone," Meg said.

"Of course not. Something might happen to him."

By the time we caught up with Will, he was in the Brats' yard, talking to Brett. Neat piles of leaf bags lined their curb. Their green lawn was raked clean. Ours, in contrast, was still ankle-deep in leaves.

We watched as Will whispered something in Brett's ear. Brett laughed and swooped Will up, swinging him high in the air. "That's my man!" Brett said. Will squealed in delight.

Meg and I shouted, "Be careful! You might drop him!"

Brett only laughed again and swung Will up higher. "Do it some more!" Will shouted.

"Put him down," I ordered. "He could get hurt."

Brett ignored us. "Come on, monkey," he said to Will. "Let's show them our trick." He knelt down, and Will climbed up on his shoulders. Then Brett got up, and slowly Will stood up.

I held my breath as Will balanced himself. Slowly he let go of Brett's hands. "Ready? One, two, three!" Will launched himself into the air. Brett caught him and lowered him safely to the ground.

I let out my breath, feeling weak all over.

"You idiot!" Meg yelled. "What if you'd missed?"

"Brett never misses," Will told us. "We practiced and practiced over a big leaf pile. His daddy used to do it with him, and he did it with Bobbie until he got sick."

"Who's Bobbie?" Meg asked.

"My brother," Brett said quietly. "He died of leukemia when he was about Will's age."

"Oh." Meg looked embarrassed. "I'm sorry . . . I didn't know . . ."

I felt terrible. There just couldn't be anything worse than losing a tiny little brother.

"It's okay," Brett said. "We're all kind of . . . well, used to it now. Not that you ever get used to it, really, but . . ."

We stood there a moment, not knowing what to say. Then Will tugged at Brett's hand. "Swing me again. Swing me way up high!"

Brett looked down at him. "You really are a little monkey, aren't you? I'm going to take you out to the jungle"—he swooped Will up—"and find you a whole troop of chimpanzees to play with." He tossed Will in the air and caught him easily.

That funny tingly feeling washed over me again. I couldn't stop looking at Brett. He was pretty big for thirteen. His father was a lobsterman, and maybe Brett helped out on the boat. Maybe that's where those muscles came from. He handled Will gently, with a calm sureness. Maybe it wasn't so dangerous after all.

I took a deep breath and tried to get back to

feeling normal. "That's enough, Will. We have to go."

"Look out," Meg whispered to me. "Here comes Bratty Bart."

Brett gave Will a final toss, then passed him to me. Will scrambled down immediately.

"Hey, Nut-Meg," Bart called, pushing a lawn mower toward her. "Now that you're all lathered up, should I shave you?"

"Very funny," Meg said.

"You know what?" Bart's grin was enough to drive anyone crazy. "I just rode past the school, and *you know what*?" He paused, but Meg refused to say anything. "There was a whole bunch of girls out there on the field, kicking a little black and white ball around."

"Oh no!" she screamed. "I forgot soccer practice! The coach will kill me!" She ran to the garage for her bike.

"Why didn't you just tell her?" I asked Bart. "Why'd you have to be such a jerk about it?"

"We don't call her Nutty-Meg for nothing." He bent over and pulled the cord on the lawn mower. The motor pop-popped, then roared.

"Oh yeah?" I shouted over the noise. "Well, just you wait! We've got a little surprise for you! We've got a surprise for the whole neighborhood! The whole town will get a surprise!"

"Yackety yack," Will sang.

"Not now, Will!" I grabbed his hand and

dragged him home. He wouldn't speak to me for hours because I'd been fighting with his friends, the Brats.

It turned out to be easy to tell Mom about the flamingos. For one thing, Meg and I had dinner all ready when she got home, then we waited for just the right moment, after Will was in bed. For another, Mom was the sort of person who didn't get uptight about things like front yards. In fact, she preferred the natural look.

She used to argue with Dad about crabgrass. "It's green, isn't it? The poor crabgrass has as much right to grow as any other kind of grass." She also thought dandelions were pretty, especially in the puffball stage.

Of course, there's nothing natural about a flock of putrid-pink flamingos in a Connecticut yard, and that's where serendipity made a difference again. This time it was a combination of Mrs. Gundy across the street, Dad, and Mrs. Wexford, the PTA president.

"I'm not sure your plan will work," Mom said, taking a sip of coffee. "But I'm tempted to say yes to the flamingos, just to see Mrs. Gundy's face when she spots them. That would give her something new to complain about."

Mrs. Gundy was over here almost every day. When were we going to rake our leaves? Good children didn't leave toys and bikes scattered all over the yard. We shouldn't allow Lady to bark so much. Mom's car was too noisy; she should get her muffler fixed. And so on.

Mom sat back and took another sip of coffee. "Back in the sixties we knew what was really important. They called us flower children. Have I ever told you about it?"

"Oh yes," I said quickly. Only about a million times.

"In those days, we didn't care about artificial things, like appearances. We knew it's what's inside a person that counts. When I lived in the commune, we didn't care that the walls needed paint, we cared about each other."

She went on, talking about peace marches and sit-ins, about Bob Dylan and Joan Baez. She was telling us about the concert at Woodstock when the phone rang.

It was Dad. We didn't get a chance to talk to him. Our ex-flower-child mother, caught up in her memories, was making a statement to society in general and to Dad in particular. Her very last sentence was, "I'm me, and I'll put flamingos in my front yard if I want to, and the heck with you, James Sullivan, and the heck with the rest of the world!"

Mrs. Wexford from the PTA called the moment she hung up. "No, I'm sorry," Mom almost snapped. "I simply can *not* bake six dozen cookies for the Open House . . . yes, I understand, but you see I work full-time and . . . I realize most of the other mothers work, too . . . but

. . . but you don't understand . . . yes, well . . . yes . . . no, I won't forget. Six dozen a week from Thursday."

She slammed down the phone. "I don't believe I said yes! I don't believe it!"

"Why did you?" Meg asked.

"That woman could talk a whale into flying! When am I going to find time to bake six dozen cookies?"

"Meg and I can help," I said.

"You girls are wonderful, but you already do so much. Besides, it's the principle of the thing! I should have said no!"

The phone rang again. This time it was Babba. I ran to the extension in the kitchen. "Yes, bring on the flamingos!" Mom shouted wildly. "All the flamingos you can find! I want wall-to-wall flamingos in our front yard!"

"Are you all right, Connie?" Babba asked.

"I'm fine! How many flamingos can you get?"

"Twenty-seven."

"Only twenty-seven? Well, it's a very small yard. Twenty-seven will be just perfect!"

"Connie, are you drunk?" Babba said.

"Of course she isn't," I said. "She just had a fight with Dad, then Mrs. Wexford made her say yes when she wanted to say no—"

"Six dozen cookies! Can you believe it?"

"Cookies?" Babba sounded puzzled.

"Never mind!" Mom shouted. "The heck with

cookies. The heck with everything! We'll have a yard full of flamingos! We'll show 'em all!"

"Yeah Mom!" I cheered.

"Way to go, Mom!" Meg added.

"Who said you can't fight city hall?" Babba said. "I'll ship you twenty-seven flamingos tomorrow!"

**6**

The UPS man was unloading carton after carton of flamingos when Meg and I got home from school Monday. The front porch was piled high with boxes.

Over the weekend Mom, trying to keep a straight face, had asked Mrs. Gundy to sign for "a UPS delivery," in case the flamingos came when we weren't home. Mrs. Gundy was in her yard now, watching the show like it was the Rose Bowl parade.

"Thanks, Mrs. Gundy," I called, waving to her. I knew she'd stick around for a while and I was dying to see her reaction.

Meg had already ripped open a box. I joined her, pulling out one pink bird after another, tossing newspaper wads right and left.

By the time the entire flock was unpacked, Mrs. Gundy was standing on our sidewalk. "Don't you think you'd better pick up those newspapers, children, before they blow all over the neighborhood?"

The yard was covered with papers. "Don't worry, Mrs. Gundy," Meg said. "We'll pick up every one."

"I see you've got some flamingos," she said.

"Yes, our grandmother sent them from Florida," I answered, jamming one into the ground. It tilted and fell over. "Aren't they super?"

Mrs. Gundy studied them, her head cocked. "Reminds me of when I was a little girl. We used to live in Florida, you know. We had flamingos like these, little gnomes, too, and the most darling little windmill . . ."

Meg and I looked at each other, too stunned to speak.

"Ah, it takes me back," Mrs. Gundy went on. "But don't you think you'd better rake your leaves first? The flamingos will look much better on a nice green lawn."

"Uh, yeah . . . right," Meg mumbled.

"They'll stand up better, too," Mrs. Gundy added, as my flamingo toppled over again.

I trudged to the garage to get the rakes.

We had half the lawn done and half the

flamingos planted when the Brats rode by. Mrs. Gundy may have disappointed us, but I was sure they wouldn't.

"Hey, look at that!" Bart braked his bike with a squeal. "Kitty-Kitty found herself some birds."

Brett made a big show of skidding to a halt. "Oh wow! That's funky! Where'd you get 'em?"

We gave the Brats a cool stare. "Our grandmother sent them from Florida."

"That's awesome. They look just like the ones in the zoo," Bart said.

Will came charging out the front door and made a flying leap for Brett. Georgie followed more slowly, showing off his badge of honor: a bandage over his cut nose.

"Did you see our plamingos?" Will demanded. "Babba sent them just for us."

Brett tossed Will in the air. "Sure we saw them. They're a little hard to miss!"

Bart looked at the pile of flamingos waiting on the porch. "Are you going to put up *all* of them?"

"Of course," Meg said.

"That's *really* funky."

Meg just stared at him.

"Can we show Georgie your trains?" Will pulled at Brett's sweater. "Can we, huh?"

"Sure." Brett tucked Will under one arm and swept up Georgie with the other. "I hear you're a wounded soldier, Georgie. What happened?"

Will and Georgie chattered happily, telling all about the tragic accident, with an emphasis on the quantity of blood spilled, as they went down the Brats' driveway.

Meg stalked up to me, her rake held like a javelin. "I thought you said these tacky birds were going to annoy the Brats."

"Can I help it if they don't know tacky from funky?"

"Well, so far your plan isn't working very well. Mrs. Gundy *and* the Brats don't hate our flamingos. They have the nerve to *like* them."

"Don't forget, we're trying to blackmail the Zoning Board. The whole point is to make them agree to Babba's apartment. They're the important ones, and I'm sure *they'll* know tacky when they see it."

We finished the leaves and had all the flamingos stuck around our lawn by the time Mom got home. Her face changed from tired to cheerful when she saw them. I have to admit, they did look colorful. We have a fairly small yard, so twenty-eight big birds made quite a crowd. They looked kind of rosy in the fading light.

"They really make a statement, don't they?" Mom said, getting out of the car. "Everyone is bound to get our message."

Mrs. Zangrilli came by. She and her husband lived with her father down at the end of our block. I'd checked with her about babysitting when we moved in, but she wasn't going to have her first baby until spring.

Today she was walking their German shepherd. Actually, you could say the dog walked her, since she didn't have too much to say about the whole process. "Hi," she called, trotting past at the end of the leash. "Getting ready for Halloween?" The dog spotted a squirrel down the street and off they went.

"Well, maybe not *everyone* will get the message," Mom said.

"It's the Zoning Board that counts," I reminded her. "They might even call tonight. But definitely by tomorrow."

Two days later we hadn't heard a word. I was going crazy. Most of the neighbors either ignored the flamingos or, like Mrs. Zangrilli, assumed they were for Halloween. Mrs. Gundy was over every day, admiring the flock and talking about her childhood, which sounded extremely boring.

Meg took it more calmly than I did. When Bratty Bart made the mistake of not hating the flamingos, she began to spend her time dreaming up new ways to annoy him.

Dad came back on a business trip and stopped in to see us Wednesday night. Will flew at him the moment he came in the door. "Daddy! Daddy! Throw me up!"

"Throw you up?" he repeated, lifting Will gently for a hug. "Why? You don't make me sick."

"Dad, that's gross!" Meg said.

"Swing me way up high!"

"Not in the house, Will," Dad said, putting him down. He came over to Meg and me. "How are my beautiful girls?" He gave us each a kiss on the cheek. "Where's your mother?"

"Right here," Mom said, coming in from the kitchen with two mugs of coffee.

"Thanks," he said, taking one. Dad was on the short and round side, with brownish hair like mine. I seemed to take after him, although I still hoped to inherit Mom's long legs someday.

"Well, what do you think?" Mom asked, sitting down in her rocker.

Dad stood by the fireplace. "About that display on the front lawn? It's extraordinarily tacky."

"That's what we want!" I said. "I knew you'd get it. The problem is, you're the only one so far."

"Of course I 'get it.' But I wish you'd taken my advice about this ridiculous idea." He looked at Mom. "Constance, you should have known better."

"Don't call me Constance," she said. "That's the last thing in the world I am—constant."

"How could I forget?" he said with a slight smile. He turned to me. "Listen, you've just moved here. Don't you want to make a good impression on the neighbors?"

"We want Babba," I said.

"I can understand that, but this scheme of yours won't work. You've just wasted your money and created a bad impression in the neighborhood."

"It will too work," I muttered.

"No, it won't." He was so stubborn.

"Yes it will! I *know* it will!"

"Don't be so stubborn, Kit."

"You're wrong! I *know* you're wrong. I'm going to *make* it work! You'll see!" I ran out of the room and pounded up the stairs. I slammed my bedroom door, then opened it and slammed it again, to make my point clear.

Faintly I heard Will's little voice drifting up the stairs, "Yackety yack. Don't talk back." Then Dad's booming laugh.

I'll show Dad, I thought. I'll show him, and I'll show the Brats, and the whole town. My plan was going to work. It just had to.

When I got home from school the next day the same feeling of fury swept over me again at the sight of those ridiculous flamingos in the front yard. I helped myself to some stale store-bought cookies and went out back where Meg was practicing her soccer dribble.

"We've *got* to do something about the Zoning Board," I told her.

"Kit, there's nothing we can do. Play goalie for me, will you?"

"Sure." I sat down on the back porch steps.

"Goalies don't sit. Stand up."

I stood.

Meg kicked the ball hard and it crashed into my leg. "Ouch! Cut that out!"

"You're supposed to catch the ball, silly."

"Well, you don't have to attack me like that." I rubbed my leg. Attack. I liked that word.

"I've got it, Meg!" I shouted after a moment.

"What?"

"If no one else will attack our flamingos, we will!"

"What are you talking about?"

"*We* are going to call the Zoning Board and complain about our flamingos. Only, of course, they won't know it's us."

"You mean, disguise our voices?"

"Your voice. Only one of us should call."

"Then you do it, Kit. It's your idea. Besides, you're a better actress."

I couldn't resist that. We went inside and I practiced about fifteen minutes, trying to sound like a stuffy old lady. Finally Meg said I was ready.

I called the Zoning Board while she went to the extension. When a lady answered, I said in a high, shaky voice, talking through my nose, "Hello? I'd like to speak to the person in charge."

There were a couple of clicks, then a man asked if he could help me. "Yes, young man, I'd like to make a complaint." I was so nervous, it wasn't hard to make my voice quiver. "I live on Pocasset Road and I am calling about those disgustingly tacky pink flamingos in the Sullivans' yard. I demand that you have them removed immediately!"

"I'm sorry, madam," the man said. "The Zoning Board has no control over any decorations people choose to put on their property."

"But . . . but . . . you're the Zoning Board! You can tell people not to build apartments!"

"That's a different matter. I suggest that if you object to the flamingos, you speak to the owners. Personally, I think they're rather funky. But you, of course," he added quickly, "are quite entitled to your own opinion."

The phone slipped from my numb fingers. Meg hurried in from the living room and hung up the receiver for me.

"Now what?" she demanded.

"This is a disaster," I whispered.

"You're darn right it is! Do you realize we spent every penny we had plus the ten dollars we borrowed from Mom—"

"She gave it to us. It wasn't a loan."

"—to buy those stupid birds and no one, absolutely *no one* minds that we have a flock of tacky, putrid-pink flamingos on our front lawn—"

"Except Dad. He minds."

"Except Dad. And we are broke—stone, cold, penniless broke—with Halloween and Christmas coming, and the neighbors don't care and the Brats think it's funky and the Zoning Board doesn't give a darn what we put on our lawn, *and* we are not one teeny-tiny-midget step closer to building an apartment for Babba!"

I thought about crying but I was too numb. Maybe later. I just stood there in the kitchen listening to Meg, wondering what we were going to do with twenty-eight plastic flamingos.

I shouldn't have worried. When I woke up the next morning, the flamingos were gone.

# 7

Meg went wild. First she blamed the Brats, then Mrs. Gundy, then Dad, then poor little Will for stealing our flamingos. Will burst into tears and Mom let the eggs cook into rocks while she tried to calm him down. As for me, I just couldn't believe my luck could get any worse.

We missed the bus and Mom had to drive us to school. It was a sunny, warm day and there were a lot of kids on the playground waiting for the first bell.

The weird thing was, everyone was crowded around the little kids' play area. When we got closer, I saw why.

Perched in the jungle gym, hanging from the swings, peeking out of the playhouse, were twenty-eight pink plastic flamingos.

It was like someone had hung up my underwear for all the world to see. I went from numb to furious in a flash.

Meg and I were out of the car and running the moment it stopped. If I'd been a hornet, I'd have stung everyone in sight.

"Who did it? Who did it?" I yelled.

A million kids stared at me but I didn't care. All I could see were those stupid, tacky birds dotted all over the playground, glowing putrid pink in the sun.

We skidded to a halt by the jungle gym. Robbie MacLean stood there, patting the head of a flamingo that seemed to be chinning itself by the beak.

"These your flamingos?" he asked. Something about the way he said it sounded odd.

"Of course they're ours!" Meg shouted.

"They're funky, man," Robbie said. "How'd they get here?"

"That's what we want to know!" I spotted the Brats over by the swings. A bird nested on each seat and more swung from the crossbars. The Brats were trying to look cool, but they were both grinning like crazy. I marched right up to them. "You did this, didn't you?"

"Us?" They looked at each other with fake innocence. "Why would we do something like this?"

"Because you're total jerks, that's why," Meg said.

"Aw, come on," Bart said. "We just felt sorry for those poor flamingos, stuck in the same lawn, day after day. We thought they needed a change of scenery, get a little education maybe."

"You stole them!" I shouted.

"They're not stolen," Brett said. "They're right here."

Mom and Will had come up to us by then. "Well, boys," she said quietly, "since the flamingos are here and they ought to be at home, I'm sure you'll be happy to help return them, won't you?"

"Uh, sure, Mrs. Sullivan," Brett said.

Most of the kids pitched in to carry the flamingos over to the car. It took a while to untie some of them from the swings and jungle gym. I couldn't get them out of sight fast enough.

When our big station wagon was stuffed with the birds, Mom said, "Brett, aren't you missing school?" His junior high started earlier than Jefferson Elementary.

"Just first period," he answered. "I have study hall anyway."

The first bell rang and most of the kids, including Bart, headed inside. Will ran off with Georgie and the other first-graders.

"I'd give you a ride to school, Brett," Mom said, "but there's not much room." We'd barely managed to cram all the flamingos in.

"That's okay, Mrs. Sullivan, I run five miles a day." He took off in a long, steady lope.

"Why are you being so nice to him, Mom?" Meg asked. "After what he did?"

"A sense of humor should be rewarded, don't you think? You have to admit, those silly things really looked funny."

"Mom!"

"I'd love to know how they managed it," she added.

Meg kicked a pebble across the driveway. "I heard Bratty Bart tell someone that Robbie MacLean's older brother has a pickup truck."

No wonder Robbie had sounded odd! He was in on the whole thing!

The second bell rang. "Hurry up girls, you don't want to be late." She looked at her watch. "Oh no, I forgot about my staff meeting! It started fifteen minutes ago!" She squeezed in among the flamingos and drove off.

School was a nightmare that day—for me. Meg, the wavemaker, surfed right along on all the attention.

It started the moment we walked in the door. A little second-grader came up to us, holding out a notebook. "Are you those flamingo girls?" Meg nodded. "Gee, the whole school's talking about you. Can I have your autograph?"

My face turned red-hot, but Meg said, "Sure. Do you have a pen?" She sounded like a movie star. The little boy handed her the stub of a pencil. "What's your name?"

"David." He was missing four front teeth.

"To David," Meg said as she wrote, "with best wishes from the flamingos and your friend, Meg Sullivan."

"Gee, thanks!" He grabbed the notebook and darted off.

"Maybe those flamingos weren't such a bad idea after all," Meg said. She turned down the hall toward Mrs. Carstairs's room, waving good-bye.

I was in Mr. Johnson's room. And so were Bratty Bart and Robbie MacLean. I tried to slip in the door, hoping no one would notice me. Some hope.

"There she is!" Robbie shouted.

"Hey, Kitty, Kitty, Kitty, you sure have pretty pink birds," Bart said.

"What'd you do, rob a zoo?" someone asked.

"Squawk, squawk!"

"It's the flamingo queen!"

"Where'd you get all those things?" Katy Stillson asked as I dropped into my seat. She had shiny dark hair and bright, curious eyes.

"Florida," I muttered.

"How come?"

"My grandmother sent them."

"How come?"

"Quiet, class." Mr. Johnson saved me. He's the

kind of teacher you listen to, whether you want to or not. But there isn't a teacher in the world, not even Mr. Johnson, that can stop note-passing. I must have gotten a hundred notes that morning and they all wanted to know why I owned a flock of plastic birds.

The problem was, I couldn't think of a single reason besides the truth. How could I say, "We bought them to blackmail the Zoning Board, only my stupid plan didn't work"? No one, especially not Katy and her friend Jennifer, would ever think I was normal after that.

The only note I answered was the one from Melissa, the snobbiest girl in the class. It said, "Did you know that plastic flamingos are terribly tacky?" I wrote a big YES across her words and passed it back.

"How come you answered Melissa's note and not mine?" Katy asked as we headed for gym.

"And mine?" Jennifer added. She was a tall, blonde girl and she echoed everything Katy said.

"Because . . ." I mumbled. "Because . . . she asked me something I could answer."

"Why can't you answer us?" Katy said.

"Yeah, why?" Jennifer added.

"Because . . . because . . ." I grabbed at an idea. "Because it's a secret!"

"It's a secret and you won't tell us?" Katy gave me a funny look. "I thought we were friends."

"We are! It's just that I . . . can't . . . tell."

"All right for you, Kit Sullivan!" Katy's bright

eyes were flashing. "You keep your secrets and we'll keep ours!" She grabbed Jennifer's arm and they walked away.

The rest of the morning was miserable. It got a million times worse when suddenly during English a thought popped into my head. Kids were sure to be asking Meg the same thing. *What was Meg telling them?*

She wouldn't tell anyone about my dumb idea, I thought. Would she? No, of course not. But what if she did? What if everyone in her class knew—and I wouldn't tell Katy and Jennifer? When they found out . . . it was too awful to think about.

The moment the lunch bell rang, I dashed into the hall to find Meg. I was moving so fast I almost whizzed past her. She'd been coming to find me.

I pulled her over to a corner. "You didn't tell anyone, did you?" I hissed.

"Tell anyone what?"

"About my stupid plan!"

"Of course not."

"Whew." I sagged against the wall. "I knew you wouldn't, but . . ." I shook my head, thinking of the disaster I'd just missed.

"Why would I tell anyone about your dumb plan? You wouldn't tell anyone if *I* had come up with a plan that stupid."

"Wow, thanks," I began. Then I thought about what she'd just said. "Thanks a *lot*!"

"Just kidding." She grinned. "Let's buy some

milk and take our sandwiches outside. Everyone in the cafeteria will be asking questions and I'm getting tired of answering them."

"Meg? How *did* you answer? What did you say when everyone asked why we have those tacky flamingos?"

"Oh, sometimes I said I was training them for the circus, and sometimes I said plastic flamingos were an endangered species and the president of the United States asked us to start a refuge for them, and sometimes I said we bought them to scare away the diddlebugs . . ."

"What are diddlebugs?"

"Who knows?" She grinned again.

I looked at my twin and wondered if we really came from the same family. "How the heck did you think up all that stuff?"

She shrugged. "It was easier than trying to remember the major exports of South America."

By the time we'd taken our lunch out behind the old oak tree in the playground, Meg was snapping her fingers again.

"What's the matter?" I asked. "Who're you mad at?"

"Bratty Bart, of course."

"Why? It seems like you kind of enjoyed being famous and signing autographs and being asked questions and all." Not like me, I thought.

"*No one* steals *my* flamingos and gets away with it."

I didn't even try to figure her out. After living with Meg since before we were born, I knew there were some things I'd never understand.

"But how come only Bart?" I asked. "I thought they both did it."

"Brett just helped," she said. "I *know* it was all Bratty Bart's idea. And he's going to pay for it."

I was secretly glad that she was leaving Brett out of it, but I didn't want to stop and wonder why I felt that way.

Meg shoved a tuna fish sandwich at me. "Here, hold this. You're my witness." She put her left hand on the tuna and held up her right. "I do solemnly swear that I will get back at Bratty Bart Bradley for stealing our flamingos. I solemnly swear I will dare him to do the most horrible thing in the world. Just as soon as I decide what that is."

"This is crazy, Meg," I whispered.

"Shhhhhh, they'll hear us."

"Turn on the flashlight. I can't see."

"Not yet."

"This thing's *heavy*. What're they throwing away, rocks?"

*"Shhhhhhhh!"*

"Ouch!" Something in the dark poked my side.

"We're there," Meg hissed. "Open the door."

I put down my garbage can and felt around till I found the side door in our garage. It opened with a loud screech.

We both froze, expecting lights to pop on, sirens to wail, searchlights to pin us like flies. But the houses around stayed dark and silent. It was a cold night and everyone must have been sleeping behind closed windows.

We lugged the two big garbage cans into the safety of the garage. Meg found another flashlight and handed it to me.

"Newspapers," she whispered. "Let's put down some papers. It'll make it easier to clean up."

We spread papers around the cans and lifted the lids.

"Phew! Fish!" I held my nose.

"I guess it makes sense. Bratty Bart's father is a lobsterman, isn't he?" Meg handed me one of Mom's rubber gloves. "You can have the right one. I'll use the left. Come on, let's get started before someone catches us."

Piece by piece, we began pulling out garbage. The Brats' family didn't tie things up neatly in plastic bags. They used grocery bags, and everything was dumped in together. Lobster shells and milk cartons and mashed potatoes and cereal boxes and fish bones and lima beans and sopping paper towels were mooshed around, glued to each other. The smell was unreal.

If you've never had a twin sister like Meg, you've probably never stood in a freezing garage in the middle of the night emptying your neighbor's garbage cans. I knew I shouldn't have made that bargain with Meg. Why don't I ever listen to myself?

"Find anything?" she asked.

I pulled out a few more objects. "Lemonade can, coffee grounds—yuck!"

"I've got a fried chicken bucket—now we know they don't have lobster every night—also a paper towel tube, *Newsweek* magazine, an envelope that says 'you may already have won a million dollars,' and a bread bag."

"What kind of bread?"

"Whole wheat."

"Boring."

"There's got to be a clue in here somewhere. Keep digging."

Meg had heard somewhere that detectives, or psychologists, someone like that, could find out a lot about a person by going through his garbage. So that's what we were doing. Looking for something that would tell her how to really get back at Bart. Weird, right?

"Hmmmm," Meg said. "Maybe I've found something." She held up three soggy cartons.

"What are they? Sara Lee boxes?"

"They're all Sara Lee chocolate cake. Let me think about it. There may be possibilities here."

I went on digging while she studied the boxes. I was nearing the bottom of my garbage can. An empty wine jug, probably from the party the Bradleys had Saturday night, a mess of bill envelopes, more lobster shells . . .

"I've got it, Kit!"

"Good!" I pulled my head out of the garbage can. "You mean we can quit?"

"Chocolate cake. All boys love chocolate cake, right?"

"Uh, I guess so."

"I'm going to make Bart a chocolate cake. An *enormous* chocolate cake."

"That doesn't sound so awful."

"It will be, if Bart's eyes are bigger than his stomach." She grinned like the Wicked Witch. "Come on, let's get this stuff cleaned up and get back to bed. We have school tomorrow."

*Now* she remembers school, I thought, throwing garbage back into the can. It was two-thirty in the freezing morning and all Meg had come up with was chocolate cake. I made up my mind that whatever her plan was, it *wasn't* going to involve me. No way, José.

As usual, I was wrong. Meg said I still owed her help because she'd spent so much money buying those silly flamingos. After school we stopped at the grocery store for two boxes of cake mix and two cans of frosting. "Let's get the cheapest," she insisted. "He'll never notice the difference."

When we got home, we scrounged up four cake pans and preheated the oven. We had the kitchen to ourselves. Mom was at work, of course, and Will was over at Georgie's. We were getting pretty good at baking by now, especially after making six dozen cookies for the Open House.

Meg cracked eggs into the cake mix. "Maybe we should add an extra ingredient. Like a powdered laxative."

*"Meg! You wouldn't!"*

"Don't get so scared. I was just kidding." I noticed that she didn't look me in the eye, though.

I watched her carefully after that, since you could never be quite sure with Meg. In the end, the only thing that went into the pans was plain old chocolate cake batter.

"How are you going to do this?" I asked as we washed up the bowls and beaters.

"We've got to have a crowd around. He won't chicken out if a lot of kids are there to see it. I checked, and his soccer team has a game after school tomorrow. I think we should make our presentation at the end of the game."

We live just over a mile from the school. A mile is nothing on a bike. A mile is forever when you're lugging an enormous chocolate cake. Of course, the fact that I wasn't eager to get there slowed things up a bit, too.

Meg had put the cake in a big box and tied a red bow around it. We took turns carrying it, but it was near the end of the fourth quarter when we arrived at the game.

The score was tied three to three with two minutes left to play. The teams ran up and down the field, with Monroe almost scoring, then Jefferson, then Monroe. Robbie MacLean blocked a Monroe pass, and bounced the ball off his head to Bart. Bart controlled the ball, dribbled downfield, then passed to Robbie. Robbie took it to the goal line, passed to Bart. Bart kicked the ball past the goalie's head. The ball whammed into the net.

Jefferson went wild. Teammates jumped all over Bart and Robbie. The crowd cheered and shouted, and Meg and I joined in. It was the first win of the season, and boy, did it feel good!

When the final whistle blew, Bart sauntered off the field, trying to act casual and cool. A crowd of girls surrounded him, including Katy and Jennifer, who were being careful to ignore me.

Meg waited for the excitement to die down a bit before she picked up the cake and marched over to Bart.

"Congratulations, Bart." She smiled sweetly. "Good game."

"Thanks." He tried to look modest but it didn't work.

"I've brought you something. But you can only have it on one condition."

"What's that?" He should have been suspicious, but he was still caught up in scoring the winning goal.

"Open it first." Meg handed him the box. "Be careful. Don't drop it."

Bart untied the red ribbon, then lifted out the cake. I must admit, it looked pretty impressive— four layers and gobs of swirly brown frosting.

"Wow, that's great! Hey guys," he called to the rest of the team. "Come and get some of this!"

"Wait a minute," Meg said. "You haven't heard my condition."

"Yeah? What is it?" He didn't take his eyes off the cake.

"It's all for you. You have to eat the whole thing. Right now."

"Right now?" He looked startled.

"Right now. The whole thing. *I dare you.*"

By this time, the team and most of the girls were gathered around us. Bart looked from one face to another. "You d-dare me?"

"I double-dare you," Meg said smugly.

He looked at the cake and turned a little pale.

"What's the matter, Bradley?" one of the boys said. "You chicken?"

"Give it to me," someone else said. "I'll eat it in one bite."

"Come on, Bradley, you can do it," another said.

Bart frowned at Meg. "What did you put in it?"

"Nothing! Honest, it's just cake. Ask my sister." She put her hand on my shoulder.

Everyone stared at me. I wished she'd left me

out of it, but I said, "It's true. It's just cake. I was there when she made it and she didn't put anything in it." Thanks to me, I thought.

Bart looked down at the cake again.

"You gotta do it, Bradley," Robbie MacLean said. "She dared you."

"She double-dared you," someone added.

Bart took a deep breath and squared his shoulders. "Of course I'm gonna do it. I was just figuring out where to start."

"Way to go!" Robbie cheered.

"What's the matter?" Bart's coach pushed his way through the crowd.

"Meg dared Bart to eat the whole cake," someone explained.

"She double-dared him," Robbie said.

The coach looked at Bart and the cake. He was a big man and he worked at the lumberyard. "The whole thing?" he asked.

"The whole thing. Right now," Meg said.

The coach shook his head, looking at Bart. "You're nuts, you know that, don't you?"

"I like chocolate cake, sir," Bart said, his head high.

The coach shook his head again. "You're going to be sick as a dog."

Good, I thought, the coach would stop the whole thing.

"We've got practice tomorrow, and the big

game against Fairfield on Friday," the coach went on. "Just make sure you're in shape to play." He turned and left.

I couldn't believe the coach was letting it happen. I couldn't believe Meg was going to get away with this.

"Okay, Bradley, go to it!" Robbie shouted.

Bart stared at the cake, then grinned. "What? No fork?"

Meg whipped one out of her pocket and handed it to him. She thinks of everything.

"Eat it! Eat it!" the crowd began to chant.

Bart tossed the fork on the ground and broke off a huge chunk with his hand. He stuffed it in his mouth. "Ummm, good," he said with his mouth full.

Chunk followed chunk. At first Bart enjoyed it, cracking jokes about what a lousy cook Meg was, and so on. After a while, he stopped with the jokes and began to concentrate on eating.

The crowd kept egging him on. "Take a bi-i-ig bite this time." "Ummmm, nice gooey frosting . . ." "Only half a cake to go, Bradley."

I began to feel sick just watching him. The more he ate, the worse I felt. The bites became smaller and smaller, his chewing became slower and slower. His face got redder and redder, then paler and paler.

Meg had been watching with a big smile on her face, but slowly the smile faded and she began to frown. "I didn't realize how big that cake was," she whispered to me.

"He can't eat the whole thing, Meg," I whispered back.

The crowd had become quiet as they watched Bart force down each mouthful.

Meg looked around, sighed, then took a step forward. "Okay, Bart, I take back my dare. You can stop now."

He shook his head, pointing to the rest of the cake. His face was smeared with chocolate and his eyes were kind of wild.

"You don't have to finish, Bart," Meg said. "I made the cake too big."

He shook his head again and broke off another bite.

"She's right, Bradley," Robbie said. "You'd better stop."

"Yeah, enough is enough," someone said.

"Come on, Bart," Katy said. "You're gonna kill yourself."

Bart forced down another mouthful, and Nature settled the question right then and there.

Watching someone lose his lunch—or cake—is not a pleasant experience. We sort of drifted away, to give him some privacy.

When it was all over, Meg pulled a clean towel out of her jacket and went over to Bart. "Here."

She handed him the towel. "Look, ah, I didn't know it'd be like this . . . this bad, I mean."

Somehow he managed to give her a crooked grin. "Just wait," he croaked. "Just wait till I come up with a dare for you."

# 9

The Monday before Halloween was so warm and sparkly it felt like spring. Meg had soccer practice so I was watching Will and Georgie after school. We'd stored the flamingos in the old tent, but the boys had collected all their cars and trucks and wanted to turn the tent into the "Amapolis 500."

I said it was okay, but they'd have to empty the tent themselves. I had a new Richard Peck novel I couldn't wait to start.

"Kit! Come quick, Kit!" Will shouted. "The plamingos are gone!"

I ran out back. Will and Georgie had pushed

open the tent flap and there wasn't a flamingo in sight. Oh well, I thought, so what? They weren't much use to us anyway. Besides, it was such a nice day, I didn't have the energy to get mad.

Not Will. He was furious. "Somebody stole our plamingos! I'm gonna catch that robber! I'm gonna call the police!"

He ran toward the house, but I blocked his way. Will almost never got mad, but when he did, he was like a hurricane. The best way to deal with it was to distract him quickly, before he got going.

"Hey, Will, guess what?" I knelt down, holding him firmly by the arms. "I'll bet it's all a joke, like before. I'll bet the Brats—I mean Bart and Brett"—Will hated it when we called them the Brats—"took them, just to surprise us."

"Yeah?" He looked hopeful.

"Yeah. And I'll bet they're going to bring them back real soon." I tried to think quickly. "I'll bet they're bringing them back right now, only . . ." Only what? I wondered. "Only, ah . . . they're waiting for us to get out of the way."

"Why?" Will demanded.

"So they can bring them back! I've got a great idea! Let's take a picnic to the beach. We'll have a good time, and when we get home, all the flamingos will be here."

"You promise?" He looked at me with big eyes.

"Well . . . I can't really *promise* . . . but I'm sure that's what will happen." And if it didn't, I thought, Mom would be home from work and *she* could deal with Will.

"Can we take cookies?" Georgie asked.

"Sure, and juice," I said.

"And bananas," Will added.

Crisis over, I threw the food and my book into a backpack and the three of us, plus Lady, headed for the beach.

You can't see our beach from the road, because of the sand dunes. Georgie and Will ran ahead of me, up the path over the dunes. When they reached the top, they let out whoops and yells that sent Lady into a fit of barking.

I hurried to the top of the path. Spread out along the beach, shining in the sun, were our flamingos. They faced the water and were arranged in small groups, like they were the real thing. For the first time, they didn't look tacky. They almost looked beautiful.

Quite a few people were on the beach that day and most of them were collected around the flamingos. Will and Georgie raced down the dune, with Lady close behind. I followed more slowly, not quite sure how to deal with this.

By the time I caught up to them, Will and Georgie had proudly informed everyone that the silly birds were ours. A lady with a camera seemed especially interested.

Will pointed to me. "That's my sister. She got Babba to send them!"

"Hi," the lady said. She wasn't very old,

maybe in her twenties, with long dark hair and freckles. "I'm Mary Beth Callahan. I work for the *Clark Harbor Crier.*"

"You mean the town newspaper?" I asked.

"Yes." She had a friendly, relaxed way about her. "How do you happen to have so many plastic flamingos?"

"Babba sent one plamingo," Will piped up. "And Meg and Kit spent all their money to buy a zillion more so Babba could come live with us."

The lady smiled at him. "I'm not sure I get the connection."

Will was such a blabbermouth. I took off my backpack to distract him. "Here's our picnic, Will. Aren't you hungry?"

"Cookies!" Georgie shouted.

"And bananas!" Will grabbed the pack and began rooting through it.

"Who is Babba?" the lady asked me.

"Uh, she's our grandmother," I said.

"Can you explain what your little brother is talking about?"

"Ah . . . I'd rather not," I muttered.

"Come on, it sounds fascinating." She had such an easy smile.

"It's too embarrassing," I said, jabbing the toe of my sneaker into the sand.

"I'm not asking because of the paper," she said. "I won't print anything if you don't want me to. I'm just curious, that's all."

"Look, Miss Callahan—" I began.

"Call me Mary Beth." Her eyes crinkled at the corners when she smiled.

All of a sudden I really wanted to tell someone the whole stupid story. It was like, if I told this Mary Beth person about it, the whole thing would go away and stop bothering me.

"Well . . ." I paused. "Cross your heart you won't tell anyone?"

"Cross my heart and hope to die."

We left Will and Georgie with their picnic and walked along the beach while I explained my brilliant, crazy, dumb plan. Mary Beth seemed so interested it wasn't that hard to confess.

When I finished, she stood quietly looking out at the water. A tanker crept along, way out on the Sound. Two seagulls flapped into the wind, then wheeled and sailed back over the waves.

"You know," Mary Beth finally said. "There might be a way to make your plan work after all."

"How do you mean?"

"I'm sure you've heard the phrase 'power of the press'?"

"Yeah, sort of."

"I'm thinking that if we printed your story—"

"*Print it?* Oh geez! I'd die!"

"Wait a minute, let me explain. I think if the whole town knew how much you wanted your grandmother to come live with you, you might arouse a lot of sympathy. People are always willing to help the underdog, and the Zoning Board has caused a lot of problems for a lot of people."

"I don't get it. How would that make the Zoning Board change its mind about building an apartment for Babba?"

Mary Beth looked down at the camera swinging from her neck. "I've covered a few Zoning Board meetings for the paper. I'm no expert, but I know you have to prove 'hardship'—that's what they call it—when you appeal a Zoning Board decision."

"What does that mean?"

"In this case, it might be possible for you to prove that it's a hardship for you, and your family, to be deprived of your grandmother's care and company."

"You really think so?"

She tapped her camera. "Like I said, I'm no expert on the Zoning Board, but I do know what the power of the press can do."

We started back up the beach while I thought about it. I was beginning to feel excited. Maybe my plan wasn't so dumb after all. Maybe there really was a way to make it work.

But maybe people would just laugh at me. Katy and Jennifer would sit together at lunch, giggling and pointing at me. I might spend my whole life eating all by myself, banished to some lonely corner of the cafeteria.

But, what if my plan *did* work? What if I made the Zoning Board change its mind? I'd be a hero—not too many people beat the Zoning

Board. Maybe they'd even put my name on a plaque in Town Hall.

*And* we'd have Babba here with us. I thought of her laugh and her arms, always ready for a hug. I thought of coming home to a warm house with the smell of dinner cooking, and clean laundry in the drawers, and homemade cookies for dessert. Most of all, I thought about how happy Babba would be to be with us.

Boy, would Dad be surprised! I'd told him my plan would work. Now I had a chance to prove it.

"Okay," I told Mary Beth. "You can print the story."

"Great!" She threw her arm around my shoulder. "Let's get some shots of you and your brother with the flamingos."

Georgie insisted on being in the pictures, too, so we all posed until Mary Beth ran out of film. A large crowd watched, but when they asked questions Mary Beth just said to be sure and get Thursday's paper.

When Mary Beth and the other people left, I discovered we had twenty-eight big plastic birds on the beach. How was I going to get them home?

"Need some help?" Brett appeared out of nowhere.

My stomach jumped around a little. "How did you get here?"

"Walked." He pointed at Bart coming toward us from the dunes. "We watched the whole thing from up there."

"Brett!" Will made a flying leap and Brett caught him in mid-air. "Kit said you'd bring the plamingos back."

"That's why we're here, monkey," Brett said, giving Will a toss. "Don't want them to get washed out to sea."

The sun was low in the sky by now, and the tide was creeping in. Water swirled around the legs of one flamingo and it toppled over.

I rescued it and said to Bratty Bart, "Is this supposed to be your way of getting back at Meg?"

"Nope, I'm still working on that." He grinned. "This is just for fun. Thought your water birds might enjoy a day on the beach. Too bad Nutty-Meg wasn't here to go crazy."

"You won't like this," I said, gathering up more flamingos, "but you guys may have just done me a big favor."

"What do you mean?"

I smiled mysteriously. "You'll find out when you get Thursday's newspaper."

Bart shrugged and went off to collect flamingos. Brett looked at me for a moment, those blue eyes dancing. "What's up?"

I suddenly felt breathless and tingly all over. I couldn't say a word. All I could manage was another smile, which I suspect looked more sickly than mysterious.

"Look, Brett." Will pointed. "A plamingo is drownding."

Brett went to fish the bird out of the water. But first, he winked at me.

I stopped breathing altogether.

# 10

The *Crier* arrived on every doorstep in Clark Harbor on Thursday afternoons. And everyone in town read the *Crier*, we discovered, when Meg and I took Will and Georgie trick-or-treating that night.

*And* everyone recognized us, even though Will was a lion, Georgie was a skeleton, and Meg and I were covered in sheets. We hung back in the shadows when the boys went up to the doors.

"Oh, you poor little darlings," Mrs. Gundy said, smothering the lion in a hug. "Now don't you children worry." She looked straight at where Meg and I were trying to hide behind a tree. "I'll be a second grandma to you, you dear, sad little children."

Mrs. Merritt dropped a handful of chocolate kisses in each bag. "I wasn't too crazy about those flamingos, but now that I understand, I don't mind a bit. What harm can a little apartment do?"

"No use trying to fight the Zoning Board," Mr. Baker grumbled. "They got steel where their hearts should be."

"The minute I read the paper," Mrs. Walsh said, "I called Bob Hutchins—he's the head of Zoning, you know—and I gave him a piece of my mind, I can tell you."

At Mrs. Zangrilli's, her father answered the door wearing a wizard's hat and a black robe. He was kind of old and very tall, with a white beard that looked real. He'd dressed up their German shepherd, too, in a cape decorated with stars and moons. The dog sat there quietly, keeping an eye on the candy.

"I built myself an apartment out back when my wife died. That was long before they told me I couldn't. Looked into my crystal ball"—he pointed to his hat, smiling—"and saw all those rules and regulations sprouting up like weeds."

By the time we reached Georgie's house, I felt really mixed up. It was awful to have so many people knowing about us, but it was nice that everyone seemed to be on our side.

Meg and I helped Mrs. Kirsten check over the

boys' Halloween candy, then she gave us each a caramel apple while Will and Georgie sorted, counted, and traded their loot.

Mrs. Kirsten handed me several copies of the *Crier.* "These are for you. I bought lots of extras so I could send clippings to all our relatives. It's a good picture of Georgie, don't you think?"

Smack in the middle of the front page was Mary Beth's photo of Georgie, Will, and me— plus the flamingos, of course. Above it a big, black headline said, GIRLS IMPORT FLA- MINGOS TO FIGHT ZONING BOARD.

I'd already read the article about fifteen times. Mary Beth had written it like a regular news story. I mean, she didn't make fun of us, or try to be cute or anything. She got our names and ad- dresses right, too.

"How does it feel to be famous?" Mrs. Kirsten asked.

"It's great!" Meg said. "It stinks!" I said at the same time.

Mrs. Kirsten laughed. "You'd better get used to it, Kit. You're going to be the talk of the town for a while."

Meg bit into her apple. "I can't wait to hear what the kids in school will say."

I groaned. "I'm not going to school tomorrow." I didn't even want to *think* about it.

The phone rang. It was Mom, asking for me. "You and Meg had better come home right away and stick those flamingos up in the front yard.

I've been going crazy! People are driving past and when they don't see those silly birds, they come to the door and ask for them!"

"You're kidding!"

"No, I'm not! And the phone's been ringing off the hook. Between the doorbell and the phone— *plus* the trick-or-treaters—I'm going out of my mind!"

Will didn't want to leave, until Meg and I promised to let him help replant the flamingos. We hurried home. Sure enough, a car was parked in front of our house, full of little kids in Halloween costumes.

A large lady at the front door was saying to Mom, "But I promised the children if they didn't eat all their candy tonight, I'd take them to see the flamingos."

Mom spotted us coming up the sidewalk. "Thank goodness you're here!" She turned to the lady. "If you'll wait just a few minutes, my daughters will bring out the flamingos."

"Well, it's about time," the lady huffed. "It's a school night and it's getting late, you know." She stomped back to her car.

"Can you believe some people?" Mom asked, shutting the door behind us. She still had on her apron from fixing dinner, and her hair was flying out in all directions. "Put down your candy, Will, and help your sisters. Hurry up, girls."

"I *am* helping," Will said. "Kit 'n' Meg said I could!"

The phone rang and Mom went to answer it. We raced out to the tent in the dark backyard and began hauling out flamingos.

"This is crazy," I said as we carried armloads of plastic birds to the front yard.

"It sure is," Meg said. "Who would have guessed people would come out *at night* to see these dumb things?"

We put Will in charge of sticking the flamingos in the ground while Meg and I went back for another load. When we returned the lady was trying to buy a flamingo from Will for fifty cents.

"They're not for sale," Meg told her.

"But you've got so many," the lady said. Her kids were running all over the yard, pulling up flamingos and playing catch with them.

"They're not for sale," a male voice repeated behind me.

I whirled around. "Brett!" My heart beat faster with surprise. At least I think it was surprise.

"Need some help?" Bratty Bart was just behind his brother.

"Not from *you*," Meg snapped.

"Yackety yack," Will began to sing, but the lady interrupted him.

"Okay, I'll give you a buck," she said. "And that's my final offer."

"The flamingos are not for sale, ma'am," Brett repeated very politely.

"Well! If my money's not good enough for

you . . ." She yelled to the kids, "Darleen, Jason, all of you, get in the car right this minute!"

It took her forever to round them up, but finally they were all inside the car. The lady got behind the wheel, slammed the door, and drove off with a roar.

Meg began to giggle, then I did, and Will chimed in. Before we knew it, the Brats were laughing with us. A group of late trick-or-treaters went past on the sidewalk, watching us suspiciously.

Mom opened the front door. "Are the flamingos set up?" Then she saw the pink birds scattered around the dark yard. "What's going on?"

"It was that lady and her kids," I said between chuckles. "But we'll set them up now."

"I've just had a call from Mr. Hutchins." Mom shivered in the cool night air. "He's the head of the Zoning Board. He said that because of all the publicity, they're scheduling a special meeting to hear our appeal a week from Wednesday."

"You mean it worked?" I couldn't believe my ears.

"Well, at least they're going to listen to us."

"Hooray!" I shouted, throwing a flamingo in the air.

Meg caught it and tossed it up again. "Three cheers for the flamingos!"

Brett caught it this time. "Careful! This here's valuable property. Don't want to damage it."

"Right," I said. "This pink thing and its friends are going to get our Babba up to Connecticut!"

"Kit," Mom said. "The Zoning Board's going to listen to our appeal, that's all. It doesn't mean they'll decide in our favor."

"They will! I know they will!"

Mom shivered again. "Just remember," she said going back inside, "don't count your chickens . . ."

". . . before they're hatched," I finished for her. "That's one of our grandmother's sayings," I told the Brats.

"Yeah, well, maybe we should be counting flamingos instead," Bart said. "Come on, we'll help you put them up."

This time Meg didn't object, but as we stuck flamingos around the yard, I wondered why Bart was being so nice all of a sudden. I found out as soon as we'd planted the last one.

Bart rammed it into the ground, then said, "By the way, Nut-Meg, I've got a dare for you."

I heard her suck in her breath. "Oh yeah? What?"

The porch light shone on Bratty Bart's cocky grin. "I dare you . . . I double-dare you . . . to kiss Robbie MacLean in front of the whole school."

Meg screamed.

# 11

"Why didn't he dare me to hijack the school bus?" Meg wailed as we got dressed for school the next morning. "Or—or steal an elephant from the zoo? Or swim across the Atlantic Ocean? That stuff would have been *easy*."

"It's just a little kiss, Meg." I crawled under the bed looking for my yellow sweater.

"In front of the whole school! Everyone's going to think I'm a pervert."

"Lots of girls kiss boys." I found my overdue library book, a bunch of old homework papers, and my favorite sneakers, but no sweater. I backed out, banging my head on the metal bed-frame.

"Kissing's gross!" She pulled an orange turtleneck over her head. "And so's Robbie Mac-Lean!"

"Hey, do you think he knows about the dare?" I tried the closet. Maybe my sweater had fallen down somewhere behind all the junk.

"Who, Robbie? Who cares?"

"I'll bet he doesn't know."

"It would serve him right for helping Bratty Bart take the flamingos to school. Aren't you dressed yet? Hurry up or you'll miss the bus."

I pulled my head out of the closet in time to see her disappear. Now I knew where my yellow sweater was. Over Meg's orange turtleneck.


It was bad the day the flamingos went to school, but I knew it would be ten times worse this Friday. I'd thought about faking a stomach ache, or trying the old thermometer-under-the-hot-water trick, but that stuff hadn't fooled Mom in ages. I finally decided just to get it over with.

The moment I got on the bus I wished I hadn't.

"There they are—the flamingo freaks!"

"Oh wow, the famous bird twins—I'm sooooo impressed."

"Some people will do anything to get their names in the newspaper." That was from snobby Melissa.

"Hey, Nut-Meg," Bratty Bart called from the back of the bus. "Those birds are superfunky."

A girl in front of him yelled, "My Dad said the last time the Zoning Board changed their minds was when the dinosaurs wanted to improve their swamp."

"You wasted your money," someone said.

"Poor little baby girls want their grandma," someone else chanted.

"Stop it!" Will stood in the middle of the aisle, stiff with anger. "You just stop it! Leave my sisters alone!"

Everyone must have been just as surprised as I was. They all shut up.

Mrs. Rinaldi, the bus driver, spoke before they could start again. "Everybody sit down and be quiet. You know the rules. Besides," she added, shutting the door, "the ones who behave themselves get a treat." She held up a bag of Halloween candy.

That did it. The rest of the ride was bearable. I watched Will sitting with Georgie across the aisle. For the first time, I noticed his chubby cheeks had melted away and his face had a thinner, more grown-up look. The sleeves of his new jacket were already a little too short and his pants didn't quite reach the tops of his scuffed-up sneakers.

"Hey, Kit." Meg spoke quietly in my ear. "When do you think he'll make me do it?"

"Do what?"

"You know," she whispered. "The dare."

"Oh. That. I don't know." Here we were, about to face a schoolful of teasing and all Meg was thinking about was one little kiss. Kissing was nothing. They did it in the movies all the time. I wondered what it felt like.

Meg snapped her fingers. "It's the waiting that's the hard part. He said I had to do it, but he didn't say *when*."

"We have Assembly this afternoon. He'll probably want you to do it then."

She turned white. "In front of all the teachers?"

"He said 'the whole school.' I guess that includes teachers, too."

She made an odd noise somewhere in the back of her throat.

"Hey, come on," I said. "It's not so bad. Really. You've taken dares a hundred times. Remember when you climbed all the way to the top of the old maple tree in the cemetery?"

"You mean when I broke my arm?"

"It wasn't your fault that branch was rotten and fell off. And remember when Kevin dared you to jump across that big stream behind the church and you did and you didn't even get your shoes wet?"

"Yeah, but I got everything else wet when I fell back into the water."

"But your shoes stayed nice and dry up on the bank. And Kevin had to admit that counted."

She began to perk up so I went on reminding her of the good old days until the bus arrived at school.

Katy and Jennifer were standing by the front door, scanning each bus as it emptied. Right away my stomach began to ache for real.

Meg and I stayed in our seats until most of the kids were off. Just as we were about to get up, Bratty Bart came down the aisle.

He bent down over us. "Today, Nut-Meg. At Assembly. I'll fix it." He strolled toward the front of the bus.

She turned pale again, so I said in a disgusted way, "He sounds like he's been watching too many detective shows."

She just looked at me.

"Come on, Meg, you can do it. A kiss only takes a second."

She made that odd sound in the back of her throat again. I sighed and said, "This is one of the times I wish we were identical twins. I'd rather switch with you and kiss some stupid old boy than face Katy and Jennifer."

Meg began to come alive again. "What's the matter with Katy and Jennifer?"

"They're mad at me because I wouldn't tell them about my plan, and now the whole town knows about it, that they'll probably never speak to me again."

Meg jumped up and headed toward the front

of the bus. "If they give you a hard time, I'll take care of it."

That's my sister, I thought, following her out. She could handle anything—except a kiss.

Katy and Jennifer ran up to me the moment I got off the bus. "We've been waiting for you!" Katy shouted.

"Hey, leave her alone," Meg said.

"What?" Katy looked confused.

"I said leave her alone."

"But I just—"

"I'm warning you—" Meg began.

I interrupted her. "It's okay, Meg." She looked surprised. "Really, it's okay. I'll see you later, all right?"

Meg shrugged. "Sure. Later." She walked off.

"What's the matter with her?" Katy asked.

"Nothing," I said quickly. "Listen, Katy, I'm sorry . . ."

"Sorry?" She seemed puzzled. "What are you sorry for?"

"You know, for not telling you about my plan."

"Hey, it's okay. I know why you had to keep it secret. Because of the newspaper, of course. Me and Jennifer, we're sorry we got mad at you."

"You are?"

"Yeah, and we think it's a terrific plan. You're really smart to think of it." Katy grinned.

"I am?"

"Yeah." Jennifer gave me one of her shy smiles. "It's a really neat idea."

I smiled back, feeling warm inside. "You know what? I think it's going to work, too. Mr. Hutchins from the Zoning Board called last night and said they're going to have a special meeting a week from Wednesday."

They wanted to hear all about it, so I told them everything that had happened as we walked to our room. The moment we got there, I got ragged on, and of course there were a million really dumb flamingo jokes, but I didn't mind too much because I was going to sit with Katy and Jennifer at lunch, and after school they were coming to my house to see the flamingos.

By the time lunch was over, I'd just about forgotten Bratty Bart's dare. When the PA system announced it was time for Assembly it all came back in a rush.

Poor Meg, I thought, as we filed into the auditorium. Her class was already in and I could see her copper-red head shining a few rows from the back. She glanced around, saw me, and tried to smile. She looked miserable.

From my seat between Katy and Jennifer, I saw Bratty Bart say something to Mr. Johnson, who nodded. Then Bart went over to Mrs. McCafferty, the principal, standing near the stage. She listened to him, frowned, shook her head, listened some more, then shrugged and nodded. Bart came back to his seat looking pleased with himself.

Mrs. McCafferty went up on stage to the microphone and tapped it a couple of times. "Testing one-two-three-four. Ah, it works. Good afternoon, boys and girls. Today, Miss Hurd's third-graders have prepared a wonderful program for you. They're going to sing some songs and perform a little skit entitled *How Handsome Mr. Toothbrush Beat Old Mr. Decay.*"

A groan went up from all the bigger kids in the back of the auditorium. Mrs. McCafferty gave us one of those looks that principals are famous for. The groans stopped.

"But first," she went on, "three sixth-graders have an announcement to make. Please come up, Bart Bradley, Meg Sullivan, and Robbie Mac-Lean."

Robbie looked surprised. Very surprised. He stood up slowly and Bart gave him a push toward the stage. Meg was still in her seat, slumped down like she was trying to fade into the wood.

Bart went over to her and, taking her arm, practically dragged her to her feet. Robbie was standing in the middle of the aisle, watching Bart with a puzzled look. Pulling Meg behind him, Bart pushed Robbie ahead and somehow got them up the steps and onto the stage.

Meg stood there, her head down, looking like the end of the world had come. I felt tense all over, wishing there was something I could do to help her.

Bart placed Robbie near Meg, then went to the

microphone. "Meg Sullivan has something to show you," he announced.

The whole auditorium got quiet, waiting for Meg to do whatever she was going to do.

Meg just stood there a moment, looking at the floor. Then her shoulders went back, her head came up, and I saw that special sparkle in her eye.

She walked a couple of feet over to Robbie, who now looked terrified.

Very slowly, very gently, she bent over and kissed Robbie on the cheek. He turned bright red and the audience burst out in screams and hoots and yells and whistles.

But Meg wasn't finished. Snapping her fingers, she marched over to Bart, who was laughing the loudest. Since he was still in front of the microphone, you could really hear him.

Meg reached up with both hands and grabbed Bart's head, turning his face toward her. Like an eagle dropping down for the kill, she swooped in and kissed him right on the mouth.

It was the loudest, fattest kiss you ever heard in your life.

The roomful of kids went wild. Even the teachers were breaking up. Mrs. McCafferty stood halfway up the steps, trying to look furious and shaking with laughter.

Bart looked like he'd been shot with a stun gun. He turned totally green. Then he looked around and saw the whole world laughing at him and he began to go through various shades of red until he reached cherry. *Then* he made the mistake of looking at Meg. That's when he started back to green.

Meg didn't say a word. She just turned and walked off the stage like a princess, smiling.

# 12

Instead of taking the bus, Katy and Jennifer walked home with me after school. It was one of those crispy, blue-sky days when you just have to be outside. Meg had detention, of course, but Will and Georgie decided to tag along with us.

When we turned the corner to our house, I saw a lot of cars and people on our street. Ever since Assembly, everyone had been so busy talking about Meg and Bart, I'd forgotten about the newspaper story.

"Hey, they're looking at our plamingos!" Will shouted. He and Georgie took off at a run.

"Wow, what's it like to be famous?" Katy asked.

"I don't know," I said. "I'm not used to it yet."

"I've never known anyone famous before," Jennifer said softly. I'd begun to realize that the reason she sounded like Katy's echo was because she was usually too shy to speak for herself. But now she seemed to be relaxing with me a bit.

When we got close enough for Katy and Jennifer to see the flamingos, they stared, just like everyone else.

"There are so *many* of them," Katy said.

If we'd had a large front lawn like we'd had in Treaton, it wouldn't have looked like such a lot, but twenty-eight big birds crowded into our little yard was really . . . well . . . supertacky.

"There she is," someone said, pointing at me. "That's the girl in the newspaper!"

Heads turned and eyes stared at me. "Uh, no," I stammered. "It's not me. I mean, I'm not her. She's—she's—she's my twin sister."

"Oh, sure," a guy in greasy blue jeans said.

"It's true! I do have a twin, don't I Katy?" I grabbed her arm and squeezed it.

She looked startled. "Uh, well, ahhhh . . ."

"Will!" I spotted him sitting on the front steps with Georgie, enjoying all the attention. "You tell them. I do have a twin sister, don't I?"

"Sure." He grinned.

"See? That's my brother. He knows," I told the

crowd. Then I whispered to Katy and Jennifer, "Come on!"

They followed me as I hurried down the driveway, up the porch steps, and in through the back door. My key stuck in the lock again and I nearly screamed.

"I'll do it." Jennifer took over and the key slid out. She handed it to me. I slammed the door shut.

"What's the matter, Kit?" Katy asked. "Why did you lie out there?"

"I didn't lie." I slumped down in a kitchen chair. "I do have a twin."

"But she doesn't look anything like you."

"It's just that I hate it when all those people stare at me. And next they'd start asking questions, and . . . well, I just hate it."

"I know what you mean," Jennifer said. And she did, too.

"Thanks." I smiled at her. "Anyway, do you want some juice or cookies or something?"

"Sure." Katy looked around the kitchen while I went to the refrigerator. "Gee, your house is small, isn't it?" I could tell she didn't mean it like an insult.

"Yeah," I said, pouring lemonade. "That's why we have to build an apartment for Babba over the garage. There's just the kitchen, dining room, living room, and three little bedrooms. Meg and I have the biggest one, Mom has a small room, and Will has a tiny place the last owners used as a closet."

"Don't you have a basement? You could make that into an apartment."

"No basement and no attic." I handed out cookies. "Come on, I'll show you."

The tour of the house would have taken about a minute and a half except that I stopped to pull down the shades in the windows facing the street. The crowd outside had gotten bigger. I could see Will and Georgie out there talking to people, having a great time.

We ended up in my room. I decided to temporarily forget Mom's rule about no food in the bedrooms.

"How come you want your grandmother to live with you?" Katy put her glass on the night table and flopped down on Meg's bed. "I've got two grandmothers and I wouldn't want to live with either of them."

"I don't have any." Jennifer sat down at my desk.

"Babba is really special. She's beautiful, for one thing, and she's so much fun—she always has a quote for every situation. And she gives great hugs, and well, with Mom working, it would be nice to have someone here when we get home."

"I know what you mean," Jennifer said. "My mother works too, and we have a housekeeper, but that's not the same as a grandmother."

"My mom doesn't work," Katy said. "But I

wish she did. She's always yelling at me—oh no! I forgot to call and tell her I was here!"

"Me, too!" Jennifer said. "My housekeeper, I mean."

They went down to the living room to call, and I heard them whispering when they finished. Katy was the first one back into my room. "We need to make a plan," she said. "Jennifer and I want to help you get your apartment built."

"And I know some of the other kids will, too," Jennifer added.

"You really mean it? You'll help me?"

"Sure." Katy grinned. "If she lives with you, maybe your grandmother can stop Meg from kissing every boy around."

We burst into howls of laughter. Of course everyone knew about Bart's dare by now, but every time anyone mentioned it, we all broke up again remembering that scene—especially Bart's face.

When we calmed down a bit, we spent the rest of the afternoon making plans. It felt wonderful to have best friends again.

That night Mrs. Zangrilli's father, the man in the wizard costume on Halloween, came over to talk to Mom. It turned out his white beard was real. He was a retired lawyer and knew about the papers and plans we had to get ready for the Zoning Board meeting.

"I'll never get this all done by a week from Wednesday," Mom said after he left.

"Maybe Babba could come up and help you," I suggested.

"But she has her job."

"I bet she'd come. She wants this apartment as much as we do."

"I don't know . . ."

I ran to the phone. "Let's ask her."

We called and Babba said yes! "I'll catch the first plane after work tomorrow. I've got some vacation time I can use, and my friend Martha will take care of Daffodil. She adores that cat."

"This is so super, Babba!" I said. "I can't wait to see you!"

"I'll be with you in less than twenty-four hours!"

We all went to the airport to meet her. When Babba walked out of the tunnel from the plane, she looked so tall, so elegant, with her beautiful white hair and her just-right clothes, that I could hardly believe this was my very own grandmother.

"Babba!" Will squealed. He ducked through the crowds and flew straight toward her.

Babba knelt down right in the middle of the airport and gathered up Will in a hug. The people behind her flowed around them, smiling.

I was there right after Will. Babba's hug felt so good.

Meg had her turn, then Mom, and we all talked at once as we headed for the place where you collect your luggage.

Babba's voice was low and kind of musical. "I hate to say it," she laughed as we waited for her suitcases, "because everyone does, but my goodness, how you children have grown."

"I'm in first grade!" Will said.

"I know. You're such a big boy now." She kissed him on the cheek. "Meg, your hair has darkened just a bit to a beautiful shade of auburn."

Meg blushed with pleasure.

"Kit, you're turning into a very pretty young lady."

Me? Pretty?

In the car on the way home, I decided Babba must need glasses. But I felt happy about what she'd said anyway.

I took the couch that night so Babba could have my bed. Meg and I were going to take turns, but I was so glad to have Babba here I was ready to sleep on the couch every night.

Mrs. Zangrilli's father came over the next morning to explain more about what we had to do to get ready for the meeting.

His name was Charles Stuart, which Mom had told me was also the name of an English king in the olden days. When he walked into our kitchen that Sunday morning, he looked like a king, he was so tall, so dignified.

When Babba got up to shake his hand, I

watched the two of them standing together with the sun pouring in the door behind them, and for a moment I could almost picture a crown on my grandmother's head, too.

# *13*

The days before the Zoning Board meeting went so fast, it seemed like all I did was blink and time disappeared.

Bratty Bart had disappeared, too. Mr. Johnson told the class he was home with the flu, and since half the school was absent with the same thing, no one wondered about it.

Except Meg.

"Do you really think he's sick?" she asked me one night when we were doing the dishes. Mom, Babba, and Mr. Stuart were going over papers in the living room, as usual.

"Who, Bart?" I rinsed a plate and stuck it in the dishwasher.

"Of course Bart. I don't think he's sick. I think he's too embarrassed to come to school."

"That's crazy. Of course he's sick."

"But we don't even see him around his house. And we're right next door."

"He probably has to stay in bed."

"Maybe . . ." She filled the rice pot with water to soak.

"Meg?" I finally got up my nerve to ask her something I'd wanted to ask for a long time. "What—what did it feel like? You know, to kiss him?"

"Gross!"

"Is that all? Just . . . gross?"

"Well . . ." She went pink. "It was mostly gross, but a little bit . . . ah . . . well, maybe, uh, exciting, too." She turned back to the sink and attacked the broiler pan. "I don't want to talk about it."

She wouldn't say another word.

The next issue of the *Clark Harbor Crier* had tons of letters about our apartment. Some people were for, some were against, but they were all sure *they* were right. The phone rang constantly and people drove past all the time, staring at the flamingos. Mr. Stuart was at our house every day. I wasn't sure how I felt about that. He and Babba spent a lot of time together and I didn't really want to share her, but I knew Mr. Stuart was trying to help us.

When he and Babba and Mom talked, they used all kinds of legal-sounding words like "variance," "self-created hardship," and "waiver." "Setting a precedent" seemed to be our biggest problem.

Mr. Stuart tried to explain it to me one night at dinner. "A lot of people are afraid that if you are allowed to build your apartment, then everyone else will want to build one, too. The beach area is already too crowded, and some people will claim the apartment is for a relative but they'll rent it out to strangers instead."

"That's not honest," I said.

"Unfortunately, not everyone *is* honest. That's why the Zoning Board has to be so strict. It's going to be very hard to overcome this objection. Our main hope is to get enough support from the public to put pressure on the Board."

"A lot of people are on our side," I pointed out.

"Yes, and we've been talking to the mayor and members of the Town Council. Your grandmother," he touched Babba's hand, "has definitely made a good impression."

"Now, Charlie," Babba scolded.

"She wowed 'em all," Mr. Stuart said. "But the Zoning Board was very clever to set our appeal date so soon. We may not have time to build up enough support."

"Can't we change the date?" I asked.

"I tried. They won't budge. We'll just have to do everything we can and hope for the best."

Katy, Jennifer, and a few other kids showed up one afternoon and we munched on popcorn while we painted signs on poster board. The plan was to collect some more kids and picket Town Hall the night of the meeting. Babba stepped over and around us for a while, fixing dinner, until she finally chased us out of the kitchen.

After everyone left, I went outside. Brett was in his driveway, hosing down his father's van. A faint smell of lobsters, or fish maybe, hung in the air. Will sat on the grass, watching.

"How's Bart feeling?" I asked, walking over to them.

"Okay. He's going to school tomorrow." Brett aimed the hose at a hubcap.

"Did he get the homework I brought him?"

"Yeah, he said to say thanks for nothing." He grinned. "But what he really didn't like was Meg's flowers."

"Flowers? What flowers?"

Will was suddenly beside Brett, tugging at his jacket. "Throw me up, Brett! Throw me up!"

Brett gently pried Will's fingers loose. "Not yet, monkey. Wait till I finish the van." He turned to me. "The flowers Meg sent. The yellow ones."

This was news. I couldn't picture Meg sending Bart flowers, except maybe dead ones.

Will began to edge away, moving the way he does when he's trying to look invisible, like when he's broken something or eaten a whole bag of cookies. I began to understand.

I went after him. "Will, what did you do?"

"Nothing." He wouldn't look at me.

"Come on, baby, tell Kit." I urged, taking his hand.

"I'm not a baby!" He jerked his hand away, raced up the porch steps and banged in through the back door.

I followed him into the kitchen, but he was gone. Babba was slicing vegetables while pots bubbled away on the stove. The whole house smelled delicious.

"Babba?" I asked. "Did you take Will to buy some flowers?"

"Kit, dear, will you stir the biscuits for me?" She pointed at a mixing bowl. "Are you talking about the little tornado that just whirled through here? Yes, I helped him buy flowers for a sick friend. I thought it was very considerate of Will to think of such a thing. My goodness, that child is growing up so fast."

He certainly was, I thought, stirring the biscuits. I could see it as clear as day. All he had to do was go to the Brats' house, hand the flowers to whoever answered the door and say they were from Meg. Simple.

Will hated fighting. He wanted us to be friends

with the Brats. So he did something about it. He was right; he wasn't a baby any more.

I meant to tell Meg about the flowers, but she came home mad because her soccer team lost the game. Mr. Stuart stayed for dinner, then we both had lots of homework, then it was bedtime. I would have told her after the lights were out but it was my turn on the couch and she was upstairs with Babba.

Mornings were always crazy at our house, with everyone fighting over the one bathroom, and sneakers and homework disappearing, and all of us racing to make the bus. I really began to worry when I saw Bart waiting at the bus stop, but he just said, "Hi, Meg; hi, Kit. Hey, Will, how's my man?" He looked kind of pale.

The bus arrived a second later and we got on. It wasn't till it started that Meg hissed at me, "*What did he call us?*"

"Nothing. What's the matter?"

"He called us Kit and Meg! Not Kitty, Kitty or Nut-Meg. *Kit* and *Meg*."

I couldn't tell her about Will's flowers right there on the bus. It wasn't the right time. As a matter of fact, I couldn't seem to find a right time. The longer I waited the worse it got. I knew she'd explode like a volcano, and with the Zoning Board meeting about to happen, things were getting tense at home. Hot lava wouldn't help the situation.

Then all at once, it was Wednesday night and time for the meeting. After dinner there was a loud discussion with Mom over whether Meg and I should wear skirts or pants. We lost, of course. Will couldn't fit into the suit Mom bought him last Easter so he wore cords and a sweater, exactly what I'd wanted to wear.

We all piled into Mom's station wagon. Mr. Stuart drove because Mom said she felt too shaky. So did I. My stomach was jumping around, my fingers and toes twitched, and I felt kind of wobbly all over.

We arrived at Town Hall. Katy, Jennifer, and about twenty other kids were marching back and forth out front, carrying their signs: DON'T BE TURKEYS—LET BABBA STAY (that's because Thanksgiving was coming); KIDS NEED GRANDMAS; THIS IS A FREE COUNTRY, EVEN FOR GRANDPARENTS; WE LOVE BABBA (that was my idea); A GRANDMOTHER IS AN INALIENABLE RIGHT (Jennifer thought of that one but it took us forever to find the word in the dictionary).

Mary Beth Callahan was there with her camera, and so were some other photographers. Mr. Stuart wouldn't let us talk to anyone. He hurried us through the door, down a hall, and into a large room.

The place was wall-to-wall people. Most were strangers, but I saw a few faces I knew: Mrs. Gundy, Mr. and Mrs. Zangrilli, Georgie's mother.

Some of the teachers from school were there, too, including Mr. Johnson. I hoped he wouldn't make me write a report on the meeting.

I couldn't have anyway. The whole thing was a blur. All those legal words kept being tossed back and forth; papers and charts and diagrams were held up and passed around; Mr. Stuart and some people at a table kept talking and the audience kept shouting out and interrupting.

The room got hot and stuffy and flashbulbs kept going off. I kind of shut it all out, then from nowhere I heard my name.

"Kit!" Meg poked me. "That's you. Stand up."

"What?" I scrambled to my feet.

"Kit," Mr. Stuart said, "would you come up here and tell these people why we are appealing the decision?"

I walked up to him in slow motion. He turned me so I wasn't looking at the audience, just the Zoning Board members. They didn't look mean or bad, just very important.

I couldn't say anything.

"Go on, Kit," Mr. Stuart said. "Tell them why we want to build the apartment."

My mouth was so dry my tongue wouldn't work. One of the ladies at the table smiled at me, like she knew how I felt.

Mr. Stuart put his arm around me. That helped. "Go on, Kit. Tell them why you want your grandmother to live with you."

"Because . . ." I croaked. "Because we need

Babba!" After that, words flowed out of me. I think I told them about Hansel and Gretel, the flying goldfish; and about how Mom had to work so hard all the time; and about coming home to a house that was warm and smelled good; and about Babba's hugs and her laugh, and how she was beautiful and how I loved her very, very much.

I'm not sure exactly what I said, but when I finished the whole room was silent. I turned to go back to my seat, and for a moment I thought the ocean had roared into the place.

People were cheering. Everyone was applauding. I looked out over the mass of bodies, and along the back wall I saw Katy and Jennifer, and two blond heads. Bart was clapping like crazy. Brett smiled and winked at me.

Every little part of me did its own little dance. I was scared, surprised, embarrassed, happy, and confused all at the same time. Then somewhere deep inside, a warm glow began and spread all through me.

I stood there looking out at all those smiles and clapping hands and decided that sometimes being famous wasn't so bad after all.

# 14

Some of our friends came back to the house with us to wait for the Zoning Board to call with their decision. Bart and Brett were there with their parents. Katy and Jennifer wanted to come too, but Katy's mom took them both home since it was a school night. They were all excited because their pictures were going to be in the newspaper.

Mr. Stuart's daughter, Mrs. Zangrilli, was there with her husband, and Georgie's mother, and Mrs. Gundy, who hadn't complained about anything for days. I didn't even mind too much when they all told me how much they liked my "speech." Mom brought out some cheese and crackers and drinks, and pretty soon we were having a party.

Everyone seemed to be having a good time, except Bart. He sat over in a corner and didn't talk to anybody. I went over to him. "You don't have to stay if you're still feeling sick."

"It's not that," he said.

"What's the matter?"

"Nothing." He looked down at the carpet. "It's just that it's not fun anymore."

"What isn't?"

"You know."

"Know what?"

"*You* know. Meg." He crushed a cracker in his fist. "This mushy love stuff stinks. It was her turn for a dare, too."

I nearly choked. "You? Meg? Love?"

He stood up. "I don't want to talk about it."

He walked away and I stared after him. Where did he get that idea? Will, of course. It had to be Will! Besides the flowers, what else had he done? Or said?

I looked at my little brother. He was sitting in Babba's lap, half asleep, his head against her shoulder. His long legs dangled almost to the floor. He'd be too big for laps soon, I thought.

That was the problem, I realized. Part of him was still a baby who wanted to cuddle in a lap, but the other part was a little boy who wanted to grow up. Meg and I wanted to keep him a baby, but Will was smart.

Boy, was he smart! He was smart enough to figure out a way to stop Meg and Bart from fighting.

But they weren't *really* fighting, were they? It was really just a game, and they both wanted to keep on playing. I wondered why it had taken me so long to figure this out.

I went over to Will and knelt down beside him and Babba. "Will, you're such a big boy now. You're growing up, aren't you?"

He nodded.

"You know what?" I put my hand on his knee. "I think you're big enough to walk yourself home from Georgie's house."

His angel smile lit up his face.

"Of course he's big enough," Babba said. "My goodness, it's only a few blocks."

"And Will, you're big enough to learn to ride a two-wheeler now. I'll teach you. And maybe Meg can teach you to play soccer, too."

"Brett already did," Will said.

"Did what?"

"Teached me to ride a two-wheeler."

"*Taught* me," I said automatically, but I felt anger boiling up in me. Brett had no right! Before I could really get mad, though, I had to finish what I'd started.

"Okay, it's good Brett taught you." I could

barely make myself say the words. "And I think you're big enough to understand something important. You know how it looks like Meg and Bart are always fighting?"

Will nodded, his eyes big.

"Well, they're not really fighting. Can you keep a secret?" He nodded again. "The secret is they really like each other. They're just playing a game."

"Like soccer?"

"Yes, like soccer. Meg is on one team and Bart is on the other, and it's just a game."

"So it's okay?"

"Yes."

A tension I hadn't even noticed seemed to go out of Will. He smiled and leaned back against Babba. "That's good," he said sleepily.

"Kit, that was wonderful," Babba said. "You're a very clever girl."

I felt my face go hot. "Aw, come on, Babba." I got to my feet, then bent down and kissed her quickly.

"Run along now and let this child sleep," was all she said.

I looked around for Brett but didn't see him. Meg was over by the fireplace and Bart was by the kitchen door.

I chose Meg first. "Bart says it's your turn for a dare and he bets you can't come up with one."

Before she could explode I walked over to Bart. "Meg says she's thinking up a dare so horrible no one in the whole wide world can do it, especially you."

I left them glaring at each other and went into the kitchen. Brett was standing beside the refrigerator, talking to Mr. Stuart.

"There she is, the star of the evening," Mr. Stuart said, taking my hand. I wondered why grown-ups always said things that weren't true. "Star," "pretty," "clever." That wasn't me—was it?

"Umm," I mumbled, trying to change the subject. "How come the Zoning Board hasn't called yet? Isn't it taking an awfully long time?"

"The longer the better." Mr. Stuart held a glass of red wine up to the light. "It means some of them are in favor of us, some against. More chance of us getting the apartment. Speaking of your grandmother, I came out here to get her this wine. Mustn't keep a lady waiting. Excuse me." He moved into the living room.

I whirled on Brett. "You have a lot of nerve!"

He looked startled. "What do you mean?"

"Teaching Will to ride a two-wheeler behind my back!"

"Oh."

"He's not *your* brother!"

"I know." Brett stared into his Coke.

I listened to the words I'd just said. Will wasn't his brother. Bobbie had been his brother. Brett didn't have Bobbie any more.

Brett frowned at his Coke, like he was counting

every bubble in the glass. I knew that frown. I'd frowned like that before, when I was trying not to cry.

I took a deep breath. "He's not your brother. But I'll share him with you."

Brett looked up at me. I didn't know that blue eyes could be so *blue.* They were exactly the color of the ocean on a hot summer day. After a minute he said, "Will's pretty coordinated, you know. He'll be good at sports."

"Just don't let Meg catch you teaching him soccer." I grinned.

"You kidding?" Brett pretended to sound scared. "I'd be crazy to mess with her temper." He smiled. "I like quiet people like you."

"Me, quiet?" I began to laugh. Then I re-ran his sentence in my head. I stopped laughing and stared at him. He was still smiling at me.

That funny, tingly feeling swept over me again. This time I kind of enjoyed it, though.

The phone rang. I must have jumped a mile. For a moment I'd forgotten there were other people in the world.

"The Zoning Board?" Brett asked.

I nodded. "Probably."

He gave me a thumbs-up sign and we rushed into the living room with everyone else to hear the Zoning Board's decision.

Mom picked up the phone, crossing her fingers up high so everybody could see.

"Hello? . . . yes, speaking . . . oh? . . ." She

half-turned away from us. "Yes . . . no . . . yes, I understand . . . I understand . . . of course, thank you." She hung up.

We didn't have to ask. The Zoning Board wasn't going to let us build the apartment.

Mom gave a small shrug. "Well, we tried."

I felt like I'd turned to ice. Babba couldn't stay with us. I'd lost Babba. No Babba.

Everybody began to talk at once. "Heck of a good try . . ." "No heart." ". . . did your best." ". . . was so sure the mayor . . ."

"Attention, everyone." Mr. Stuart stood beside Babba's chair. Will was sound asleep on her lap. "May I have your attention?" We all got quiet.

Mr. Stuart stroked his beard. "As you all know, our chances of winning this appeal were not good, in spite of our efforts. And, as you all know, I'm a man who likes to be prepared. However, I was not prepared for this lady." He smiled down at Babba. "She swept me off my feet, I don't mind admitting."

"Hush, Charlie," she said, looking up at him.

"So I've given a lot of thought to various ways we could keep this lovely lady in our neighborhood," Mr. Stuart went on.

"Dad," Mrs. Zangrilli said, "we could rent her the spare room in our house, at least until the baby comes." She patted her round stomach.

"I've thought of that," he answered. "But I've also thought of a more permanent solution." He knelt down by Babba's chair. "Barbara, would you marry me?"

"M-m-marry you?" Babba stammered. She looked totally surprised—almost as surprised as I felt.

"Marry me," he repeated.

"But the children . . . Kit . . . Meg . . . Will . . ."

"You can be here whenever they need you." He tried to look fierce. "Don't want a woman underfoot all the time anyway."

"Marry you?" Babba said again slowly.

Mr. Stuart looked at her with so much love I couldn't stand it. I burst out, "Marry him, Babba!"

"Yeah, marry him!" Meg shouted.

Mom said quietly, "Do you love him, Mother?"

"Love him?" Babba said in wonder. "Of course I love him." She suddenly seemed to grow more beautiful. "And of course I'll marry you, Charlie."

"Alllll riiiight!" I shouted.

We had such a celebration then, I thought the house would burst apart. I was so happy I could have jumped up and touched the moon. Mom brought out champagne for the grown-ups and someone put romantic music on the stereo and everyone kept congratulating Mr. Stuart and Babba.

After a while I went over to where Meg was sitting on the stairs. "Hey, my plan worked after all, didn't it?"

"Yeah, I guess it did, in a weird way." She half-smiled.

"What's the matter?"

"Nothing. I don't feel so good. Remember when I kissed Bart?"

"Sure."

"I think he gave me the flu."

"Oh no!"

"It's okay." She grinned. "While I'm home sick I'll have lots of time to think up a *really* horrible dare for him."

And she did.

# ABOUT THE AUTHOR

**LOUISE LADD** didn't know she wanted to be an author until she was (technically) grown up. She tried many jobs, including working in a funeral home, before she took a course in writing for children. One of her assignments, a short story called "The Magic Umbrella," grew into her first book, *A Whole Summer of Weird Susan* (Bantam Skylark, 1987), with tremendous help and support from her friends in the D.C.A. Writers Workshop, who continue to scrutinize every word she writes.

*The Double Fudge Dare* is based on a newspaper clipping given to the author by Cindy Kane, about a man in the Midwest who successfully blackmailed his neighbors with pink plastic flamingos. Unfortunately, Connecticut zoning boards are a little tougher to fight.

Ms. Ladd is a graduate of Westtown School and Wellesley College. In addition to writing she works part-time in the Darien, Connecticut, library, acts in local productions, and produces a summer theater. She lives with her family in Connecticut in a town not unlike Kit and Meg's Clark Harbor.